DANGEROUS REFUGE

CORRUPT BLOODLINES
BOOK TWO

LYDIA HALL

ALSO BY LYDIA HALL

Series: Spicy Office Secrets

New Beginnings || Corporate Connection || Caught in the Middle || Faking It For The Boss || Baby Makes Three || The Boss's Secret || My Best Friend's Dad

Series: The Big Bad Braddock Brothers

Burning Love || Tell Me You Love Me || Second Chance at Love || Pregnant: Who is the Father? || Pregnant with the Bad Boy

Series: The Forbidden Attraction

My Mommy's Boyfriend || Daddy's Best Friend || Daddy Undercover || The Doctor's Twins || She's Mine

Series: Corrupt Bloodlines

Dangerous Games

BLURB

The handsome, mysterious man will protect me and my son under one condition... I have to marry him first.

Something draws me to Allie Clarke, and it's not just her sweet, innocent beauty. It's also her fierce desire to protect her son and her belief that people are good deep down...

As wrong as she is, Allie holds out hope for me. She doesn't know what I've done, and what I *will* do to keep her safe.

But Allie has a secret - an ex, the father of her son, who is on the hunt. He won't stop until he finds her, and she won't stop running until she's safe.

Rules we set ourselves are broken. I shouldn't touch Allie, but I can't resist anymore.

Once her ex reappears, two things are put to the test.

My loyalty to the bratva... and my love for Allie.

My decision might end us or give us the new beginning we've been craving… But no matter how I decide, when I do, it's going to change *everything*.

DANGEROUS REFUGE is the second book of The Corrupt Bloodlines series of interconnected standalones.

This is a dark spicy romance novel that can be enjoyed alone or binged with the rest of the series!

1

ALLIE

Nothing this entire night has gone my way. Standing next to the fryer in the kitchen, I dab my red apron with a towel, trying to get the grease splatters off it. I hate waiting tables, but it's the only job I could get at the time, and now the only thing I'm experienced in. Moving nine times in the past five years has meant nine different jobs, nine different apartments, nine times explaining to my son that things have to change again. I really want this to work out, but I really don't want to keep dealing with rude customers like the one who just wiped his fried chicken down the front of my apron just to prove how greasy the food was.

"Jerk off again?" Dana asks, slinging her tray into the large sink to be washed. She better than anyone knows how rude these people can be.

"Yeah, this time they smeared their food down my apron. I've about had it." I shake my head and toss the towel to the side. I'm going to wear this stain until I get home because I don't have a way to wash it out here.

"Looks like the cute guys at table six aren't giving you a hard time at all." She wags her eyebrows as she gets a clean tray and adds plates of food from the line onto it. When it's full, she leans her hip against the stainless-steel table and crosses her arms over her chest. "You need to get you a good-looking, rich man to be your sugar daddy. Then you don't have to keep doing this job."

"Yeah, well you have a boyfriend. Why do you stick around here?" My sarcastic comment bounces off of her without an answer as I pick up the tray of drinks I need to deliver to said table of gentlemen, who—if I do say so myself—are extremely good-looking. Only one of them is wearing a ring too, despite a few of them being more mature than me.

I carry the tray into the dining room, avoiding the very rude customers as they pack up their things to leave. I won't get a tip from that table but hopefully these handsome fellows will make up for that.

"I have that fresh round of drinks for you guys," I say, balancing the tray on one hand as I set each man's drink in front of him. The one with Dark smoldering eyes who has had his gaze fixed on me all night is at it again. He stares, drinking me in as his tongue traces along his bottom lip. I like the attention, but I know I'm no good for him. Paul will catch up with me at some point—probably soon—and I'll have to leave again. It's just the way things work.

"You're a tall drink," the man says. His voice is scratchy, like he's a sixty-year-old smoker, or maybe he screams a lot and he's just hoarse. But when he speaks it sends a warm rush of arousal through me. He's the best-looking one at this table in my opinion, permanent five o'clock shadow, dark wavy hair he has slicked back, and blue eyes that promise I'd be in for a pleasurable time if I flirted back.

"Thank you, but I'm not really looking for anything right now."

It's true; I'm not. I can't. Not with Rico needing me to keep him away from his father. Paul will come after me; I will be forced to move. If I start something up with a guy, I'll just want to stay, and then what will happen? Rico's father will win, and I can't let that happen. Not after what happened to us.

2

"You know, the best things happen when you're not looking for them. Just ask Dom over there." His eyes dart at the man with salt-and-pepper sideburns. He looks stern, grumpy even, not at all like this man who is speaking to me now.

"I appreciate that advice," I say as I set his glass in front of him and his eyes trail over my curves. It makes me tense, my pussy tingling a little because of the attention. I haven't had sex with a man in five years— dildos don't count and they don't cut it either. I just can't break down and have a one-night stand either. I'm too principled, too picky.

"Has anyone ever told you that you have an amazing figure?" He leans back and studies me. "You see women out there trying to do all these crazy things to make themselves more attractive to men, but you have this natural beauty." He gestures the length of my body and all I can think is how on earth does he think this ugly pinstriped waitress uniform is attractive.

I'm covered in grease. My hair is falling out of my bun. I have a run in my hose. My makeup is probably smudged from sweating too much, and I know there are bags under my eyes from lack of sleep and worry. He's either the smoothest talker who just wants a quick bang and run, or he's blind.

"Thanks, but no thanks." I am not rude at all. I don't want to be mean to anyone. I just can't let myself feel that. I can't be flattered by him—I am, but I can't allow myself to respond to it. "Can I get you fellas anything else?" I ask, stepping back.

"How about your number?" another one of them says. "Sven is lonely and he's really a good guy if you give him a chance."

I sigh and shake my head. "I'll be back with the check in a bit."

I walk away feeling lighter. It's nice to be admired and wanted, but it will only lead to more heartbreak for me. I have a feeling that I'm just going to be a lonely cat woman when Rico grows up and moves out. I'll have my ten orange tabby cats and a dozen litter boxes spread around my tiny apartment where I hide out from life in general. It's literally fate or something.

I brush my hair out of my face and force a smile as I leave behind the idea that I could escape my dreaded future by snatching up one of those handsome men. The table I'm heading to has been nothing but trouble all night, but I still have to check on them. I weave between the other patrons in the dining room with my tray tucked under my arm and force a smile.

"That potato soup is almost ready for you. I apologize again that it had bacon in it when you requested no bacon. Is there anything I can get you while you wait?"

The woman seated at the table across from whom I can only assume is her very miserable husband scowls at me. "He's already finished eating and I haven't even gotten my food. The soda tasted like syrup, no carbonation, and you didn't even bring me silverware when you seated me. I think you've done enough." Her hair is in such a tight bun it draws her eyes back at the corner, which is comical, but I don't laugh at her.

"I'm sorry again, ma'am. I'll go check if the soup is finished now." I turn, heading for the kitchen, though I would rather she just complain and leave. I'm not getting a tip from her, and she's already told my manager I did a poor job tonight so far. It isn't my fault the cook prepared the wrong potato soup, but try to convince an unhappy customer of that. I hate waiting tables when I get blamed for mistakes someone else makes.

"Sheesh," Dana says as I walk into the kitchen. "You can hear that lady all the way in here." She rolls her eyes and hands me a tray with the bowl of soup sitting in the center, complete with a new bunch of silverware and napkin.

"I know right?" I hand her my empty tray and take the one with soup.

"Look, just go give her the soup and then we'll go have a smoke or something. You need a break." Dana is sometimes a lifesaver but today, she really is.

"Did I ever tell you I love you?" I croon, offering the first real smile of the day. "Now, let me go feed the dragon."

With my back to the door and tray in hand, I back into the dining room, passing by the handsome men who let out a few catcalls. I use the boost of confidence as I approach the woman with her food. I don't know what causes it, but my foot snags on something and I lose my balance. It feels like my knees will buckle, and in order to keep my footing, I reach out and brace myself on the back of a nearby empty chair. Unfortunately, I also tip the tray holding the soup, which inevitably slides back toward me and spills down the front of my apron, drenching me in broth and chunks of potato.

I gasp, straightening as the bowl and tray fall to the ground. My apron, skirt and shoes are covered in the soup and there is nothing left to put on the table in front of her. The soup is hot, but not scalding. I quickly untie the apron and peel it off before the moistures soaks through into my shirt, but the hem of my skirt is soggy.

"Dammit," I grumble under my breath. This is exactly what I needed tonight, to make things worse with an already unhappy customer. She sees me from across the room and her scowl becomes an angry glare. Dana is there in a heartbeat with towels and I use them to dab at the sticky fabric of my skirt's hem.

"Go... I got this," she tells me, gesturing toward the woman.

My shoulders sag as I walk her way, feeling the soup soak through my ballet flats and warm my toes. It's a walk of shame. Everyone in this place saw me soil myself, and now I have to explain why this woman will not be eating her second bowl of soup.

"Was that mine! Oh my god, you're so careless. How can you be so clumsy?" The woman's tone is biting and harsh. I have to remember she is a customer not someone I know personally.

"I'm really sorry, ma'am. I—"

She stands, slamming her napkin onto the table. Her husband flushes with embarrassment but says nothing. "You should be ashamed of yourself. You know I've never had such horrible service here in my life."

"Please, forgive me. I can have the kitchen prepare you a new soup, and I would like to pay for your meal myself." I squeeze the towel in my hands. I hardly have money to pay rent, but it's the right gesture. This screw up was my fault.

"No. I want to speak to your manager." She crosses her arms over her chest indignantly and I want to smack her. I restrain myself though, knowing that will just lead to assault charges. I step backward, thinking how Karen-like this woman is being, and I run into something very firm and lose my balance again, only this time, strong hands on my hips hold me upright.

I gasp and step away, seeing the very tall, very broad-chested man from the table across the room. His dreamy eyes are focused on me for a split second then he looks at the woman. "I'm sorry, Miss. I couldn't help but witness what happened and overhear you're upset. I would like to pay for your entire meal. And I would like to leave you with a gift." He pulls out his wallet, placing two-hundred-dollar bills on the table. That's enough to pay for this meal and a few more like it.

"Well…" the woman huffs, "you are not personally responsible for this woman's failure. Are you the manager?"

"I am not. I'm just a concerned customer who wants to help." He folds his hands in front of his waist holding his wallet in them. "If that's not enough, I can offer more."

I back away as Dana walks up, shooing me. I know she's watching out for me so the manager won't get on my case, and I'm amazed how this stranger has come to my rescue. He has no reason to be so kind and bail me out of this situation with the angry woman, and I will have to thank him sometime, but right now I just want to hide.

I head for the kitchen, tossing the dirty towel into the hamper where it goes and burst out the back door with my purse in hand, snagged from the hook near the breakroom. I plop myself on the bench where I usually sit to have a smoke and pull my cigarettes and lighter out. The ground is covered in butts, probably left there by the cook. It's a gross habit, and sometimes I pick them up and put them in the trash for him, but not today. I light up and puff on the cigarette, feeling the nicotine already calming the craving I had.

I've barely gotten my cigarette lit when I see someone approaching. It's a man wearing a dark hoodie, hunched over. I stand a bit nervous, and the man folds the hood back. His dark hair and dark eyes give him away immediately.

"Oh god, what are you doing here?" My worst nightmare approaches me. Paul has found me already. I thought I had a few months left before this happened again.

"You know why I'm here, Allie. I want my son. He deserves to know his father." He jams his hands in his hoodie pockets and I drop my lit cigarette to the ground and use the toe of my shoe to snuff it out.

"I don't have time for this," I tell him, heading for the door, but he grabs my elbow and hurts me, yanking me backward.

"You better make time," he growls. "Because I am going to get my son."

"Yeah, well sue me for custody then. I'll have them drug test you and you'll go to jail. You'll never see Rico again." I wrestle to get away from him but his grip tightens.

"I'm going to get him back."

I could spit in his face right now. I'm so angry. I was just starting to settle into this new place and now he'll be following me home. "I'll never let you have him. You beat me so bad in front of him he started wetting the bed again. You're not getting him back." This is the last thing I needed today. I want to go home now and pack my things and leave.

"Hey!"

Another male voice hits my ears and I see the large man from inside charging down the alley. Paul snarls and pushes me away and I cower near the door, ready to run inside. But the large man whose name I can't remember, is at my side, standing between me and Paul in a split second.

"Keep your hands off the lady, pal."

"What's it to you, prick? This is personal business." Paul squares his shoulders. He's a near match in height and weight, but I fear the large man may go down hard if Paul hits him. I have first-hand experience with how hard he hits.

"It's my business when I see a man get physical with a woman. Now leave before I call the cops." When his chest puffs out I see the ridges of defined muscles beneath his shirt and I look away. I don't want to stand here and watch a fist fight.

"I'll be back, Allie. Rico is mine. You'll see…"

Paul walks away and the large man turns to me. "You okay?" he asks, opening the door. I nod and back into the restaurant, ready for my break to be over.

"Yeah, I'm okay," I manage to mumble. I never do get his name, though I make a mental note to try to get it if he comes in again.

He lets the door swing shut and I start a mental plan for how I'm going to tell Rico we have to move again. He'll be crushed.

2

SVEN

I lie sprawled across the gravel on this rooftop with my phone under my chin. Propped on my elbows, I stare down the barrel of the rifle's scope, my cross hairs trained on a building two blocks away. The man I'm watching has no clue I'm here invading his privacy. If he did he'd shut his curtains and not let me watch him counting stacks of cash. This man has it in for my cousin Red, and I'm not about to let him win. Not to mention the fact that he's in a great deal of debt with the family, and Dominic has called in that debt.

He moves stacks of cash from his table into a briefcase and I wonder if this is the cash he's supposed to be paying Dom with. I doubt it. He's about as underhanded as they come, double dealing with the Italians.

"Pop ain't doing so good today, Sven." On speaker phone, Leo's words hit me right in the chest. My father's condition continues to worsen just as the doctors said it would. He refuses to take the medication regularly, which I know would help him, but he's stubborn.

"He's going to die someday, Leo. We have to prepare for that. We're not kids anymore." I'm forty-two myself, and I've seen a lot of my family die, both to disease and to the pitfalls of being Bratva. It's never easy to bury someone you love, and the only way I can function is to put it out of my head. Leo is the emotional type though, hung up on sentimental things. It's the reason why he's not the one on this roof as a sniper. He'd find some way to feel pity on this bastard and fail to make the hit.

"I'm just saying things won't be the same with him gone. You know what I mean?"

"I know." I change the subject, wanting to focus on a lighter topic. Pop will die, but life will go on and I need the current of my life to pull me forward. Death has had a shadow over me for too long after Mom's suicide and the way Lacy died so suddenly. "What did you think of that woman at the restaurant? The waitress…"

Leo chuckles and says, "That redhead? She's got to be fire in the sack. Did you see how tight her ass was? Hot damn, Sven, if you can't nail that one there's something wrong with you."

I am always the butt of his jokes, Matty's too. They have never been ready to settle down because they're playboys. They like hot sex and a fast-paced relationship that ends in fireworks before they move on. I used to do that, maybe when I was in my twenties. But I met Lacy and we married quickly. Breast cancer stole her from me and I swore I'd never love again, but that waitress. There is something special about her.

"Yeah, well if you two hounds didn't chase off every woman around with your games, maybe I'd have a chance."

My comment makes him laugh harder. "You just don't have the moves like me and Matty. We play the field because a player's got to play. You know? Look man, I gotta split. You think this man's going to make his move? He seems to really have it in for Red."

I peer into the scope again, down the barrel of the gun. There is no doubt in my mind he's going to try to kill Red, but we're not going to let that happen. This asshole is going to pay for stealing from us. Red did his job by alerting Dom to the thievery.

"He's not going to get a chance. He has probably twenty grand stacked on his coffee table right now. If that was anywhere close to what he owes the family, I'd take him out right now and walk over there and get the bloody cash. I'm just biding my time until he coughs it up. Then he's mine." I lower the weapon's nose and push myself up to a sitting position. "You check out. I have something else I want to do tonight."

"You're going to spy on her again, aren't you?"

"It's not spying if I walk up to her and talk."

"Nah, then it's stalking." His laugh is obnoxious. "Hey, you seen that woman Dom has at his place? What's he doing with her?"

I recall seeing a woman at his house from a distance, but I have no clue what it's about. It has something to do with the mole we're rooting out; I'm sure of that. But Dom is secretive and he will be our new leader very soon, especially if Pop is getting worse.

"Just stay out of it, Leo. You know Dom has a temper. You're blood but blood spills easily when people disrespect their leader." My wisdom is the same to myself as it is to him. I have too many things to worry about to be snooping into my older brother's personal life. And now my mark is moving so I am free to do as I please this evening. "I'm on the move. I'll call you later."

"Sure thing." Leo hangs up and I disassemble my gun and pack it into the briefcase I carried it in. He got my mind spinning now and despite knowing nothing about that woman, not even her name, I feel compelled to see her again. Not just because she's gorgeous. Once I saw that man harassing her, I knew she needed my help, and now I will give it to her.

I head down to my car and make the short drive across town to Red's place. His car is parked out front. It's a piece of shit, but he loves that rusted-out Camry. Without knocking, I walk right in. He isn't expecting me but it's how I normally enter. He looks up from the chair where he sits watching television and nods at me.

"Want a beer?" he asks, muting the show. It's some old western shown in sepia tones.

"Nah, just here for some help. I thought I'd stop by on my way downtown for dinner." I sit on his old plaid sofa that had seen better days. Red likes to live like he's still in the sixties, not a single thing in his house updated. I sink into the cushion so far I may never get out.

"Yeah, what's that?" His hand dips into an open bag of corn chips and he pulls out a handful and shoves some in his mouth. He's busy crunching his snack while I pull my phone out and open the picture app. When that woman wasn't looking, I snapped a picture of her and the man talking.

"This woman and man, I need to know who they are. Can you do that for me? Find any information you can on them, where they came from, who they are, and what happened between them. If there is any trace of information, I need it."

"Sure," he says, nodding and chewing. Crumbs drip from his mouth onto his flannel shirt and he dusts them off. "Just send the picture and anything you already know about them."

"She works at that old diner on Seventh. The bistro place Dom likes to go to." I forward the image to his cellphone and pocket my phone again. If anyone can find out who she is, it's Red. He's a mastermind at this sort of thing and no one knows how he does it. I heard once that he has ties at the BMV but that remains unproven. "How quick can you get it done for me?" I ask, reaching past him into the bag of chips. I take a few and snack on them while he has a sip of beer.

"I don't know. Depends on what lengths they've gone to to hide who they are. If they're in the system I'll find them fast. Just a matter of scanning that image for nodal points on their faces."

"Yeah, facial recognition. Good idea." I pop another chip into my mouth and decide I'm actually hungry. I may go to that diner and see if she's there tonight. I may not need Red to find out her name for me, though I doubt she'll cough up personal information just because I ask.

"I have a few things to do for Dom though. Something about the mole. You know? I can't say much, but I'll try to squeeze this in as quickly as I can." Red sits up straighter and nods at the TV. "You can stay and watch if you want."

"Nah, I'm hungry. I'm going downtown to eat. Keep me posted." I stand and let myself out. Red and his fascination with old western's is something I've come to rely on seeing when I visit. He's just like his father, which is a comforting fact. Red's Pop was right-hand man to mine, and loyal to a fault. It's exactly what our family needs, especially with the mole pushing in on us.

I drive downtown, parking about a block from the diner. I can see her already; her red hair catches my eye. She stands down the alley next to a car. There's a blonde woman in the driver's seat and a young boy standing next to it—nine or ten years old. The redhead bends and kisses the boy on the forehead and he wraps his arms around her. There is a bit of tension in his expression, brow furrowed and eyes forlorn, but he climbs into the car. She says something to the driver and the car pulls away.

I see my opening. She's standing alone in the alley lighting a cigarette. I can approach her and have a chat, which is exactly what I intend to do. I step out of my car and lock it, securing my weapon inside where it won't be stolen. Then I head down the alley. Her back is to me, and my eyes are on that round, tight ass in the bright red skirt she wears. It's probably just a work uniform, but it is hot as fuck on her, making my dick swell the closer I get.

I'm still only halfway down the alley as I see a man step out from behind the dumpster and approach her. He's wearing a blue t-shirt, not the hoodie he had on the other night, but this is the same man who I had to chase off before. I step to the side, leaning against a light pole for a moment. Instead of rushing up to intervene, I stop and listen. I'm close enough to hear them this time, and I may glean some information from the conversation that will help me understand exactly what this woman is going through. But if he touches her, I'll gut him.

"What now?" she asks him, puffing on her cigarette. She blows the smoke away, turning her head so it doesn't go in her face. It's a polite gesture I wouldn't afford the man. His lack of respect for her proves he doesn't deserve it.

"I told you, I want my son."

"Rico is mine, and I'm keeping him away from you where he's safe." She takes a step back as he approaches. It's not dark out yet, and he's got balls if he thinks he is going to assault her in broad daylight.

"I have had to track you down nine times, Allie. I just want my kid. I deserve to be a part of his life." He wipes his mouth with a thumb and a finger and shakes his head at her. "You can't keep him from me."

"The hell I can't. All I have to do is show the court the hospital records. You almost killed me. They'll never give you custody. You'll just go to jail. Besides, you can't stay sober long enough to pass a drug test." She flicks the cigarette, sending ashes into the slight breeze. "I'm not afraid of you, Paul."

"Then why do you keep running?" His voice is thick, anger in his tone. "You seem to be all over this city and avoiding me. That's fear."

"Yeah, okay, so do you blame me? You beat the living shit out of me, then try to take my son." Allie drops the cigarette butt on the ground and stops on it, then picks it up and tosses it in the trash bin next to the door. "You need to leave me alone. I'm already searching for a new job and place to stay. You'll have to start searching again. It's never happening. You're never getting him."

She reaches for the door and pulls it open, and the man runs a hand through his graying hair. So he's abused her pretty badly, and maybe even her kid, and she's on the run from him. This jerk really has it coming to him. I would love to be the one to give it to him too. He just has to make one wrong move and I'll disappear him faster than he can blink.

I stay there, tucked behind the light pole, and he moves my direction. Allie—I like that name—handles herself well. I like that too. She's not a wilting flower; she stands up for herself. She probably had to develop that quality living with an ass like this guy. The closer he moves to me, the more I want to pound him. When he is just a few paces away, I step out and stand in his path with my shoulders squared.

"Not you again," he mumbles. "Can't you just mind your own business? What are you, her bodyguard or something?" His hands clench into fists and my body tenses, prepared to pound him if he throws a punch.

"It seems to me that Allie doesn't seem to like you visiting her workplace. Maybe you should keep your distance." I'm tempted to open my jacket and show him the piece holstered there, but I won't be the one who escalates things. That's how people get arrested.

"You have a real problem, you know? You better back off before something bad happens to you. Or maybe it will happen to her, 'cause maybe you're just a little too interested in her and I need to teach you a lesson."

God I want to murder this idiot. I peel my jacket back and flash the Ruger at him and he scowls and shakes his head. "If I see you here again, it will be the last time."

"Good luck, buddy," he calls as he walks away.

He's not intimidated by me, which isn't a problem. I don't have an ego that works like that. I know who I am and the men who stand behind me to back me up. This jerk has no clue who he's messing with. Now, I need to find out where he's staying and how to better protect Allie, because one thing is for sure, I want her. And my property will be protected at all costs.

3

ALLIE

I see him at the door waiting to be seated before he spots me, or at least I think he hasn't spotted me. I dash into the kitchen and set my tray down on the table, then watch him through the window where the cook places orders that are ready to be served. He looks around as the host leads him to Dana's section, not mine. His dark suit makes him stand out, overdressed for the little diner where I work but it fits him perfectly. I don't see him as the type of guy who would wear dockers or t-shirts. His entire persona screams money and class.

"Staring much?" Dana asks, coming up behind me. I gasp and turn around, feeling my cheeks burn.

"Not staring, just..." I can't find the words, and I can't resist turning back to watch him sit and give his drink order to the host.

"Hey," she says, leaning in beside me to look at him too, "isn't that the guy from last week? He's the one who paid that horrible woman's bill after you spilled the soup on yourself." She nudges me with her elbow. "He's hot."

"I uh…" I stammer, not wanting to reveal who that man actually is to me, the fact that he chased Paul away. In fact, he is the reason I haven't already packed up and bolted. I want to tell him thank you for helping me.

"Oh girl!" she squeals, grabbing my arm and jumping up and down. "Oh god he's so good-looking. You should totally give him your number."

Thinking on my toes, I say, "So you'll take table eight for me? I can have his table?" I peel my eyes away from his handsome face and turn to her.

"Hell yeah! You go nail that bastard. He's rich and I don't see a ring on his finger. You may just get yourself a sugar daddy." She snickered and reeled around to grab a tray and plate the food on it, and I breathed a sigh of relief.

I let her believe I'm attracted to him and that I want to date him, but really I know that's not going to happen. Not only would a man that wealthy never date someone like me, but I can't get involved right now. My interest in serving him tonight is just so I can thank him properly for watching out for me. This world needs more gentlemen to stand up for ladies around them.

I take out my order pad and a pen, and then bolster my confidence by checking out my appearance in the mirror hung on the manager's office door. I'm a hot mess like normal, but I pull off the style and make it work. My devilish red waves refuse to obey, so rather than being held tightly in a bun, they hang in wispy strands that frame my pale features. At least my makeup is fresh.

Ducking into the dining room, I weave through the tables with my gaze locked on the man. His back is to me, so he doesn't see me coming, which is better. It's less anxiety I have to feel. He is looking over a menu when I walk up, but his head lifts and a calm expression greets me.

"Well, hello there." His eyebrows rise as recognition flits across his face. "I was hoping I'd see you."

"Uh, yeah…" I stutter, already feeling like this may have been a mistake. "You were?"

"Yes, I was." He gestures to the chair across from him. "Sit down. I'd like to talk to you." His tone is formal, stern even, as if he's used to getting what he wants. But it's not possible for me to sit. I have other tables to wait on and my manager won't like it.

"I can't. I'm sorry." My hand shakes as I poise my pen and pad to take his order. "What are you drinking? And are you ready to order?"

"Allie, sit please." He nods at the empty chair and my throat constricts.

He knows my name? How could he know my name? I'm not wearing a nametag or— It hits me that he probably overheard Paul saying my name, so I relax a little and remind myself he's not a stalker. He was helpful and chased my violent ex away to save me.

"I can't really. My boss will be upset. I have other tables to wait on and the customers won't be happy if I am just sitting here when they need things." I shake my head as I'm talking but the look on his face sours, brows dipping together in the center. He's not pleased with my refusal to dine with him, but what am I supposed to do? I can't lose this job. I need the last few days of pay before I can move.

"I know Jim. It will be fine." He nods again and I glance around the room. Jim, the owner, isn't here right now, only Kyle the manager. I am nervous, but I sit, hoping this takes only a few minutes and Kyle doesn't see me here. Still, I take a peek at each of my tables where customers are eating or waiting on food. It doesn't feel right to slack off on this job even though I know I'll just be quitting in a few days anyway.

"Good girl," he says, as if he's training a dog. Part of me doesn't like being talked down to, but another part of me ignores that feeling

19

because probably the hottest, wealthiest man I've ever met wants an audience with me.

"So I get the feeling you're not here to eat." I tuck my pad into my apron pocket and fold my hands in my lap. My palms are sweaty. I don't know if it's because I'm scared of what my boss may think or if it's because this man really turns me on, or maybe a mixture of the two.

"Well, your assumption is correct. I came to talk to you." He leans on the table with his forearms and folds his hands together over his plate. When he looks at me, it does things to me, stirring my tense body. I think some women call that smolder; I just call it trouble. I can't do this. I can't get involved with someone. I'm here to thank him and serve him dinner, nothing more.

"Actually, I wanted to talk to you too." I swallow again, my throat very dry. I haven't even brought him a glass of water, so there is nothing on this table to wet my mouth with. "Uh, thank you for the other day. I mean the woman. She was so rude and that was just an awful situation."

"You're welcome."

"And thank you for what happened in the alley with Paul." I shrug one shoulder and look up at him through my thick eyelashes. "He's a real jerk. I appreciate you standing up for me." I suddenly don't know why I am sitting here thanking him. He did a kind thing and left. That was that. He could vanish into thin air right now and I'd still move on with my life. Dana has loaned me money before to get Rico dinner or pay my light bill. I thank her for things like that because we see each other five days a week. This just feels weird now. I should have said nothing.

"You're welcome, Allie. That's what I wanted to talk to you about. Are you okay? I mean does this guy mess with you a lot?" His voice lowers a notch in volume, compassion seeping into his tone. I look up at him and sigh. His eyes compel me to tell him what's happening. I have no reason to share; there is no gun to my head forcing me, but for the first time in a long time, I feel like someone actually cares.

It's not like this man can do anything to protect me or make things better, but sometimes I just need to vent. I haven't told any of my coworkers or bosses what my personal life is like, and it would be nice to just have a friend to chat with. My shoulder bobs again.

"I'm okay, honestly. I just can't stay here much longer. See, Paul was this major charmer for a long time. I got pregnant; we lived together. He was a bit physical with me, mostly during sex in the beginning, but after I had Rico he started smacking me. That turned into worse things, and when he beat the shit out of me right in front of Rico one time, I knew I couldn't stay." I look up as the door to the kitchen opens and my heart leaps into my throat, but it's not Kyle; it's Dana.

"I see. That sounds like a very tough situation." He unfolds his hands and leans back in the chair, resting a hand on his knee as he crosses his legs. "I'm Sven, by the way."

"Allie, but my friends call me Al." I feel strangely better getting that off my chest, even though I'm still on edge about my boss seeing me slacking off during work. "So now you know why he's harassing me and why I have to move so often—nine times in the past five years."

"Is that what you were telling him a few days ago?"

I look up at him, surprised that he saw me speaking to Paul again. "Thursday? Yeah, before work he confronted me again. Thank God Rico was gone already." I squint at him and shake my head. "Were you following me?"

He remains placid, unreadable. "Not at all. I just happened to be passing by when I saw him. Actually I saw you first and thought I'd approach you since I had a few minutes to spare. I find you very attractive. I wanted to speak with you, but he walked up to you first. I just walked away when I realized he wasn't going to harm you."

"So you heard me tell him to fuck off." I feel vulnerable with Sven, like he's disarmed me entirely but not in a way that is scary. Safe is the word I'd use to describe how I feel now. The idea that a man like this would find me attractive is laughable in my opinion but the words came from his lips freely.

"I did."

"And you understand why I have to quit this job and find a new one along with a new apartment yet again. That will make ten times in five years." My eyes flick toward the kitchen door again; still no sign of Kyle, but I'm not any more relaxed now than I was ten minutes ago when I sat down.

"What if there was a different way?" He leans forward again, his eyes hazing over with darkness in them, like a shadow passing over his head.

I'm not sure I understand what he's saying. A different way? I open my mouth to ask him what he means and hear Kyle's shrill tone call my name.

"Allie!"

I turn over my shoulder to see him approaching from behind me. He must have been out front not in the kitchen, and now he's seen me sitting here talking while I should be working. I pop to my feet, ashamed and embarrassed.

"I'm sorry, sir." I smooth my apron and pull out my order pad and pen.

Kyle is a no-nonsense sort of person who doesn't take shit from anyone. He may even fire me on the spot, which makes me nervous because I really need the tips I'll make the rest of this week. I still have to find another place to live.

"I'm sorry, Mr..." Kyle leans down condescendingly and purses his lips at Sven.

"Sven," he says, reaching a hand out. Kyle does not take it; instead he folds his hands in front of himself and his nostrils on his pointy nose flare out.

"Sven, our waitresses must work. They can't sit and socialize on the clock. Other customers need them. Now, if you will excuse me, I have things to do. Allie, I want to see you in the kitchen." Kyle sashays off in all of his pomp and circumstance, which is decidedly in his head, and I stand there humiliated.

"I have to go."

"He seems fun. Don't worry; I'll talk to Jim." Sven gives a soft smile and I want to ask him what he meant about a different way, but I hear Kyle call my name from the kitchen and nod at him.

"Thank you for listening to me. It felt good to get that off my chest. I've never really told anyone before."

"Your secret is safe with me, Allie. Go on before he blows a gasket." Sven returns to looking at his menu and I slump back into the kitchen to take my lecture with grace. He's such a kind man, or it seems anyway. But now I'm curious what he meant, and the entire time Kyle is lecturing me I find myself wondering what Sven meant by a different way. And now I want to see him again, just to ask him.

If there is a way to keep Paul off my back so I don't have to keep moving and running away from him, I will do it. Rico has a friend in this building and I hate that he hasn't had any real friends because we move so much. Thoughts of Sven and what he does for a living toy with me for the rest of my shift. What if he's a lawyer and knows how to make Paul leave me alone for good? Lawyers are wealthy and powerful. That would explain his fancy suits and the way he thinks dropping his name with the owner will get me out of trouble with my manager. Or I wonder if he's a police officer or something, though that wouldn't explain the money so much.

I spend the rest of my shift daydreaming about Sven and how he made me feel heard and safe. And after another lecture at the end of my shift, I apologize for switching tables with Dana and tell Kyle it won't happen again, then head home. Rico is already sleeping, curled up in bed with his Nintendo DS on the pillow next to him. I send Sarah home, thankful for such a good friend to watch my boy while I work, and I pour myself a drink.

The day has worn on me and I'm craving relaxation. I sip my whiskey as I start a bath, letting the water fill up while I smoke a cigarette and think of Sven again. Life has a way of surprising me at times, like this man. I swore to myself years ago I'd never let a man get to me, but there is something about him that just draws me and I can't say no. Like the way he convinced me to go against my conscience at work and sit down to talk with him. He has authority in his voice that I can't rebel against. Paul never had that. No man I've ever met has ever had that.

But Sven is different.

I pour a capful of bubble bath into the water and strip off, tossing my soiled work uniform into the hamper before dousing the cigarette in the toilet and sinking into the bath. The water instantly warms me and lulls me into its comforting embrace. I lay my head back and shut my eyes, and Sven is there. His azure gaze is seared into my memory, but I don't mind. Dana was right. He's incredibly attractive. I find myself picturing what he might look like without his shirt.

Then I find myself picturing what size his dick might be. Sitting across from him as he told me he found me attractive pushed some buttons, but imagining him naked in this room with me finds even more buttons to push. I slide my hand between my legs, touching lightly at my soft folds. I'm wet, no surprise there. I've felt aroused by him all day, the ache in my pussy hardly fading even during the lecture from Kyle.

I open my eyes, checking that I've locked the bathroom door, and with that reassurance, I let them flutter shut again, massaging myself. I'm so horny because of that guy, and I know nothing about him. Maybe that's even more arousing to me, that he's a mystery. I dip my fingers into my slit, feeling my sticky, thick juices collecting. I want release badly. When I push a finger into myself, the ache grows. I need it now.

As I play and touch myself, stirring up my body, I imagine Sven there, kneeling next to the bathtub with his arm submerged in the bubbles, his fingers hidden beneath the surface where I can't see them. My fingers pushing into my tight hole become his, thrusting and massaging. But it's when I imagine his voice whispering my name that does it. My body comes hard, convulsing as I fuck myself with two fingers. The water sloshes around me, and I nearly sink below the bubbles. How on earth does a man do this to me so easily?

And how can I get him to actually be the one doing it for real?

4

SVEN

Standing in the quiet sanctuary of the family bookstore, I find solace amidst the rows of books and memories. My brothers and I used to play amongst these shelves, fashioning ourselves superheroes or villains. But as I delve into the captured footage, my eyes lock onto the screen where a figure lingers outside, and a knot forms in my stomach. With every frame that plays on the monitor, my suspicions grow. The man skulking around the perimeter has unknowingly drawn the attention of Matty, my younger brother, who insists I investigate further.

The shadowed man on the recording from yesterday's overnight security camera footage is hunting, searching for someone or something. With a mole ready to take my brother down—my younger brothers have no clue—I am not taking any chances. I study his stealthy moves with one hand on my cell phone ready to call Red. The man on the footage sneaks up to the front door and brazenly tries to pick the lock, completely unaware that we have cameras watching every square inch of this property. I shake my head and dial Red's number. This idiot has it coming.

The line rings through, and after a few seconds, Red answers. "Yeah, Sven, what's up, man?"

I turn back to the monitor, watching as the intruder fumbles with the lock. He's just a small-time crook, probably looking to steal some books or cash. But I can't let him get away with it. I take a deep breath and speak with a calm and steady voice. "Red, I need you to look into something. Matty told me someone was snooping around last night. I've watched the footage, which I'm sending to you now." I quickly email the footage to Red, and I can sense Red's excitement. He's always itching for a chance to prove himself, to show off his skills. "Have a look."

There's a pause at the end of the line and I hear rustling. Red understands the sensitive nature of what's happening. Dominic has read him in on the situation with the mole; probably before he even told me. I found out about it when I overheard something I wasn't supposed to and Dom was forced to let me know what was happening. I get the feeling he wants me to stay out of the way but how do I do that if my family is at risk? So I've been handling things my own way as I can.

"Got it?" I ask, trying to move the conversation along a bit.

"Just watching it now," he says, sounding thoughtful. "Yeah, you're right. This guy needs a talking to." I sense hesitation in his voice, not the usual ambitious desire to rush into danger.

"You don't sound so sure." I pause the video on a frame when the creep looks right up at the camera, as if he's aware we're watching him and wants us to see his face on purpose. I don't recognize him, which means he most likely isn't one of our known enemies. Besides, which Italian would be stupid enough to look right into our cameras after trying to break into our building?

"I'm just saying, I don't think he means any harm."

"Means any harm? Are you an idiot?" I rake a hand through my hair, wondering what Red is thinking. "The guy deliberately tries to pick the lock on the front door of the store. He means harm. I want him taken out. Got that?" I feel my chest tightening at Red's reluctance. He knows something he's not telling me, but I don't dare question him on it, not if he's working on something for Dominic.

"Yeah, of course. I'll handle it."

"Good, now, tell me what you have on Allie." Knowing her name is a step in the right direction, and based on what I heard of her conversation with that slimeball, I gather they have a thick history. She was gracious enough to share some of the details, but I have a thirst for vengeance now. No man should ever put a hand on a woman to harm her—a little wise correction now and then goes a long way, but not abuse. Not to my property—even if it was in the past.

"Uh, yeah…" I hear more shuffling, papers rustling and the sound of Red slurping some liquid through a straw. I must have interrupted his dinner. "I got a lot. This guy Paul is a real piece of shit, Sven. The woman was in the emergency room thirty-two times in one year. She put a restraining order out on him about three years ago, but she has moved at least nine times that I can see and had about that many jobs too, all in the past five years. She's on the run from him, and I don't blame her."

While I already know most of what he tells me, the bit about her stints in the ER is news. "Tell me more about the trips to the hospital. What has he done to her?"

"It's not documented that she reported him for the abuse, but no single woman is that clumsy. And what's more, she went to different hospitals and emergency medical clinics. It's just how those things go, you know? The woman is afraid but needs medical attention, so she never goes to the same place twice. She won't draw suspicion from doctors, and the abuser keeps abusing."

"Red, the details. What did he do to her?" I'm growing impatient, chewing the inside of my cheek when I'd rather be blowing the guys brains onto the side of a building.

"Well, she's had broken arms and a broken cheekbone. At one point she was burned pretty badly, third degree on her back. She's put her back out a few times, which given her age is a little suspect. She's too young for that, so I think it's more abuse." I hear clicking in the background now, and listen intently as Red reveals the only piece of information I need. "The most interesting thing I dug up was that the man has a rep. He did three years for assault with a deadly weapon when he was in his twenties and after his release it was only six months before the hospital visits started."

"Assault?" I lean forward, feeling the butt of my gun press into my side as I plant my elbows on the desk in front of me.

"Yeah. He almost killed a man with a baseball bat, all over a dispute about a mailbox."

This guy has to be stopped. If he is this out of control, he could really hurt Allie, kill her even. "Thanks for the information, Red. Keep digging. I need to know where he's living now." If I can't stop him from stalking her, making him understand that she's under new management now, then he's going to be put down. He doesn't deserve another breath as far as I'm concerned.

"If you don't mind me asking, why do you want so much information on this guy? Usually you just shoot first and ask questions later."

Red is right. I'm impulsive, lacking self-control at times. I know it's a fault of mine. Dominic will never let me forget it. It's a vulnerability that makes him a much better leader than me. "Because I'm trying to do things the right way this time. Just get the fucking intel and stop asking me questions."

I hang up the phone before Red can pry further. I know every bit of our conversation will be relayed up the chain to my older brother and he will have things to say about it. I don't care. I saw something I want in Allie, and I'm not letting anything come between me and having what I want. I rise, smoothing my hands down my suit coat, and I feel my pistol strapped to my hip. I need to know where Paul lives if I'm going to intimidate him enough to make him leave Allie alone, or take him out, whichever seems appropriate at the time. Red is the one who is going to get me that information.

I flip off the monitor and the recording, then the lights. The old bookstore grows dim, and I make my way toward the front door in darkness. Harmless prowler or not, the man on the recording will get his just desserts and I will be rid of one more thing that distracts me from what I really want to be doing right now. I already put Tucker on Allie for the evening so I could handle this irritation. Matty was right to inform me but that doesn't mean I enjoy being distracted.

I lock up, heading to my car and decide to call Tucker to see how things are going. Allie should have been off work a while ago, and I know she walks nearly thirty blocks home to save the subway fare. I know because I've been following her, or had someone tailing her, for more than a week now. I pull my phone from my pocket and dial Tucker's number.

"Yeah, Sven. I got your girl. She's walking home from work." Tucker is moving. I can hear cars moving past him.

"Good. Any sign of the man tonight?" It's been a few days since Paul showed his face. I'm hoping maybe he got my message and he will leave her alone now, but my gut tells me he is going to strike when she least expects it. I want to be there if that happens, but when people pull me away it leaves her vulnerable. Tucker can handle himself, but I want the blood on my hands so I can taste victory.

I slip behind the wheel of my car and start my engine. I'm going to head that way and relieve Tucker of his post. I want to watch her tonight, even if I get no sleep.

"Yeah, we may have a situation brewing. I'm tailing her, but I've kept my distance. She's more than a block ahead of me with no fear at all. She hasn't looked over her shoulder once." A horn honks in the background and drowns out the next thing Tucker says.

"Say that again?"

"I said, there is a man between me and her. So far he's been distant from her. He could just be heading the same way, but I have a feeling it may be our guy. I've got my eye on her and my hand on my gun." Rex will shoot him dead in a split second, which isn't what I want. If this guy is going down, I want him to suffer the way she suffered at his hand.

"Don't do anything. I'm on my way. Just keep an eye on them and I'll meet you at her place. If he attempts to hurt her, move in, but not unless you think she's in real danger." I hang up and put my car in gear, flooring it. Allie's place is a four-minute drive in light traffic, and it's about as light as traffic is ever going to get in the city that never sleeps. I weave between two cars, punching the gas. That bastard better not lay a hand on her or I will slit his throat.

At a red light, I slow and look both directions, then blow through it. The red-light camera flashes and I know the license plate will have to be swapped out in order to make sure no one can prove my car was the one at this intersection. If I have to take drastic measures tonight, there needs to be no evidence anywhere.

By the time I am at her building, I can see her approaching at the end of the block. I shut my car off and slip out, hand on my gun. I stand in the shadows just around the corner waiting where the next building's entrance is recessed in darkness. From where I'm at, I know she will never see me watching, and neither will he. I really hope for his sake that it's not him, because I'm ready to do some damage. After what Red told me minutes ago, my blood is still boiling. I want him to pay.

I peek around the corner. She is stunning as usual, even with her hair messy and hanging loose around her face. She's let her bun out, probably exhausted from her shift. I watch her take her key from her pocket and reach for the door handle to unlock the building and let herself in. Then I see the man behind her. It's definitely her ex, and he doesn't look happy. I draw my gun, bracing myself for a fight as Tucker rounds the corner at the end of the block. In the light streaming from the window in the door, I see Allie's face flash with fear. She whips around and presses her back against the door.

"Paul! No," she whimpers just as he clamps his hand down on her mouth. She squirms and I steel myself. I can't discharge my gun here, but God do I want to. Especially when he drags her down the steps, pinning her against his body, and moves my direction. It's just the break I need.

The second he pulls her past me into the darkness created by the recessed building I act. The butt of my gun slams into his head like a cobra strike, and he relinquishes his grip on her.

"The fuck!" he screeches and drops to one knee. Before he can get up, I swing my knee upward, connecting with his jaw and I hear a sickening crack. For a second, I think I've snapped his neck, but he falls to the side, and rolls over, holding his head.

"Allie, stay behind me," I tell her, hooking my arm around her waist. She obeys instantly, crying and whimpering. She clings to me from behind, tugging at my suit coat. "You piece of shit. I told you to stay away from her." I drive my foot into his side, giving him a taste of his own medicine, and a knife drops from his hand and rolls out into the light of an overhead streetlamp. He was going to kill her.

"Fuck you, you sick fuck," he spits, trying to stand, but I drive my foot into his side, knocking him back down.

"Stay down." I plant my foot on his chest and pin him to the ground. "If I ever see you around her again, I will kill you."

Allie pulls at my suit coat, tugging me backward as I point my gun at his head. "No, Sven, please."

I go with her even though I want to peg this bastard, and she stops me at the door of her building. Tucker lingers in the shadow down the street and I nod him away. Allie glances over her shoulder, but I know she can't see him.

"Sven, I don't feel safe. I don't want to stay here alone."

"I'm here, and I'm not leaving." I holster my gun, her eyes watching my movement, and her hand trembles as she slides the key into the lock. It isn't the sort of invitation I hoped she would give me, but beggars can't be choosers. "Let's go in."

5

ALLIE

I turn the key in the lock to my apartment door and push it open, Sven following me in. The scent of pizza lingers in the air, and I know what Sarah fed Rico for dinner long before I see the empty pizza box on the coffee table. She is perched on the edge of the sofa with her phone in hand staring at the screen as I enter.

"Hey, I'm home," I say, shaken still. I drop my keys on the stand by the door and kick my shoes off. Sven enters behind me, looming over me like a cloud with his broad shoulders and barrel chest. Sarah looks up and smiles, and I watch her eyes widen as she stands. "Sarah, this is Sven, a … friend."

"Oh, hey, Allie." Sarah smooths her hands down the fronts of her thighs and shoves her phone in her pocket. "Uh, nice to meet you, Sven." Her shuffle-walk my direction is indicative of her flustered state, also evidenced by her flushing cheeks. Sarah is attracted to Sven, and why wouldn't she be? His dark hair and dazzling baby blues are a chick magnet. I have fallen to his good looks, and Sarah and I are two peas in a pod.

"Nice to meet you too," he says, completely uninterested in her hand, which she thrusts out at him. He looks around the room as he unbuttons his suit coat and walks past her. She pulls her hand back and rushes to my side, grabbing my wrist and releasing an almost silent squeal.

"Fuck, Al, he's hot." She shakes my arm and grins. "Where did you meet him and does he have a younger brother?" Sarah is clearly not into older guys. Maybe I'm not either, but Sven deserves a thank you for his trouble of watching out for me. Yes, he's hot, but I'm not looking for a relationship. I just invited him up for a drink until I settle down and then he can leave.

"Uh, he's just someone I met at work. Look, is Rico sleeping?" I pry my wrist from her grasp and she collects herself as she steps into the hallway.

"Yeah, went to bed thirty minutes ago. I checked and he's out." She wags her eyebrows at me. "Don't do anything I wouldn't do."

She says the words loudly enough that I feel my own cheeks burning and glance at Sven who has seated himself on my old, worn-out sofa as if he owns the place. His eyes are locked on me, but he doesn't seem to have heard her.

"Shh," I hiss, turning back to her. I have to stifle a snicker, and I shoo her with my hand. "I'll call you tomorrow."

Shaking my head, I shut and lock the door and Sarah, my only buffer, is gone. It's just mean and Sven now, and suddenly I feel awkward. The stack of boxes to the left of the door contain most of the contents of my life now. I have been packing for a few days, knowing tomorrow morning is when I am planning to leave. I have a hotel booked for a week, and I have a storage unit prepared for my things. My suitcase has most of my clothing; all I need to shove in it are the toiletries and I'm good, but I don't want to rouse Rico in the middle of the night. Otherwise, I'd be gone now.

"She seems friendly," Sven says, and I turn to see him drape his arm casually over the brown and red tweed upholstery. I'm nervous. He looks straight off the cover of GQ, and my couch looks like it was resurrected after the great depression and found in a dumpster. I swallow hard and slink over to the armchair on the other side of the small glass coffee table. Each move has come with its own challenges, some of them being how to furnish apartments. The leather armchair I sit in I found near the pile of garbage bags one evening on trash night. Otherwise it would be just the couch and table in this room. I don't even own a TV.

"Yeah, she's a sweetheart. We've been friends a while, but—"

"But you find it difficult to keep in touch with all the moving? She babysits for you now because you moved back closer to her side of the city?" Sven reads me like a book, challenging me to defy his knowledge. I can't; he's right.

"Yeah, actually." I fiddle with my hands in my lap. "I need a drink. You want one?" I stand again, moving toward the kitchen area of this small open-concept space. It's dimly lit and in a state of disrepair, but for just at a thousand dollars a month, it's all I can afford. I walk straight to the cupboard with no door and grab the bottle of bourbon.

"Yes, I'll have one," he says, watching me. His eyes follow my every step. I can feel them burning into me as I reach for two tumblers and pour a few fingers of the whiskey into each of them. Then before returning to sit, I down the first glass and refill it. I haven't eaten at all today, and I feel the burn all the way down my throat. The whiskey will hit me hard, but hopefully it just makes me sleep well.

"I only have plastic... I'm sorry." I apologize as I hand Sven the plastic Kool-Aid cup and sit back in the chair facing him. The table is a safe barrier. I am not afraid of him, but I am afraid of how he makes me feel—wanted. As I sip my glass of bourbon I already feel the tingle in my neck and shoulders, burning and tightening my muscles. It will only be a matter of minutes before my head begins to swim.

"It's okay," he says, but the way he inspects the cup makes me feel out of place. He is clearly very wealthy, and my home is a dump. He probably lives in a mansion.

"Look, Sven, thank you for standing up for me. I don't know what I'd do if Paul actually hurt me and got to Rico. That boy is my life." I glance at the closed door, behind which I know my ten-year-old is sleeping. "All I want to do is keep him safe."

"What If there were a way that you didn't have to leave again?" Sven looks at the boxes for a moment then back at my face. He's accurately read how soon I plan to leave.

"What do you mean?" His words linger in my head; "a different way" he'd said.

"Well I am a man of means." He sips his bourbon and watches me over the rim of the white plastic cup with the smiley face emblazoned on it. "I can keep you safe every day, just like I did tonight."

My body stirs a little. The idea that love can be contained to five sorted categories has always baffled me. It isn't through touch, words, time, gifts, or acts of service that I feel loved. To me, love has always been being safe, and Sven is speaking that language. The alcohol swirls in my head, relaxing me. I'm more open to hearing his idea of how he may keep me safe than I was when we talked at the diner, hungrier for it. I don't want to make Rico lose his friend, and I don't want to run anymore.

"How can you do that?"

"I have money and power that makes things happen. I also see something I want, and when I see something I want, I go and get it." Sven's eyes drift over my body then return to hold my gaze. All I can think about is how he tore Paul off of me, pushed me behind himself to protect me, and then threatened him. I don't fall for bad guys at all. Paul is a monster, but Sven—he used his badassery to protect me, not hurt me. That makes me want him even more. More

37

than six days ago in the bathtub when I masturbated to fantasies of him.

"You want me?" I ask him hesitantly, wondering if he means to fuck or to love. I've never had a man be so forward with me. My groin begins to ache at the thought of him saying he is interested in me, but I try to push those thoughts away. A man like this would never choose someone like me. I have to remember that he is probably playing me, and I am probably just leaving anyway. I rise, hoping to refill my glass, which I realize I haven't yet emptied. The act makes me feel foolish, so I down the contents immediately, which is a bad idea. With no food in my stomach, the alcohol is hitting me hard already. I sway and he stands, setting his glass down and reaches for me.

"Actually, yes, I do."

His hand on my waist sends shockwaves through me. I find my eyes fluttering shut as I tip my head upward. Sven's strong hand cups the side of my face, craning my neck upward as his teeth sink into my neck. "Oh god," I mutter softly, aware that Rico is on the other side of the door. "I don't know if I'm—"

"You were saying thank you?" His words cut me off and I stammer around for a way through this awkward moment, but like Moses parting the Red Sea, he comes in and blows me away with the most jaw dropping kiss I've ever had. His stubbled face scratches along mine, teeth raking over my lips, greedy hands pulling me against him. I don't' know if it's the alcohol or the fact that I find this man sexy as fuck, but I pour myself into it. It's just a kiss, or maybe sex too, but I'm leaving tomorrow. I can indulge myself, can't I?

"Fuck, Sven, not here..." I wrap my arms around his neck after he takes the glass from my hand and sets it down. The kissing continues, lips pressed against mine and tongues dancing furiously as I back toward the bathroom. He doesn't have to be guided; his hunger is obvious as he pushes me into the room, using his foot to shut the door behind us.

My heart is hammering in my chest as he takes me into his arms. His hands roam my body, setting me on fire, and I can't help but moan as his lips find my neck. I feel like I am becoming lost in him as his hands explore my curves. The way he grinds his hips against me, his hardened cock nearly bruising my thigh, I can tell he isn't just saying he wants me. He really does.

"Fuck, Sven, we have to be quiet. Rico is sleeping," I tell him, tugging at his shirt. I pull it out of the waistband of his pants and he uses his massive hands to lift me onto the bathroom counter.

"You're going to want something to keep you quiet then, because what I'm going to do to you is going to make you scream my name." Sven snatches a washrag off the counter next to me and shoves it in my mouth, followed by his tie, which he slips off of his neck and ties around my head, holding the gag in place. God, he's so fucking hot and I haven't even felt his cock in my hand yet.

I reach for his belt buckle, but he pushes my hand away. I could untie the gag at any time, but I don't want to. Every last inhibition is gone, and I want his dick inside me now. I wriggle on the counter, shimmying my skirt up over my hips as he undoes his pants and extracts the largest cock I've ever seen, stroking it a few times. "Shit," I hiss, but he can't understand me, not with the washcloth in my mouth.

"Here, let me," Sven says, sliding a finger around the crotch of my panties. He pulls so hard he rips the seam in two and makes me suck in a gasp of breath.

"Oh my god, you're so fucking hot," he says, pushing his thick shaft inside me. I am so wet I can feel it smearing all over my thighs as he pumps in and out of me. We move together, and I can feel every inch of his length as he slides in and out of me. One hand grips my hip, the other tangles in my hair, and I'm in ecstasy.

He takes his cock and slides it up and down my slit, teasing me with his slow strokes and I moan in pleasure, the sound muffled by the fabric of his tie. He grabs my hips and thrusts into me, hard and fast, and I grip the counter top, my fingers gripping it tightly.

Sven moves in and out of me, his grunts and groans getting louder with every thrust. I can feel his cock slamming up against my g-spot and I try to scream, but all that comes out is muffled moans and pleasurable sounds. The pleasure builds until it's too much, and I explode around him, my body shaking with a powerful orgasm.

"Good girl," he growls in my ear, careful to be quiet as I told him to. His hot breath on my cheek as I spasm around him intensifies my orgasm, and I whimper into the gag.

Sven soon follows, his body shuddering as he calls out my name.

The pleasure slowly ebbs away and I'm left panting and completely spent. Sven withdraws and slides down the length of my body, his hands running along my curves. He kisses my forehead before untying my gag. My mouth is dry, but my pussy gushes with his cum as he pulls out, his cock still standing tall and proud. It glistens with my moisture smeared all over it, and I feel his puddle between my legs.

Sven's eyes lock on mine and he reaches between my legs with the washcloth that just absorbed all of my pleasure sounds. He wipes me clean—hard too, not a delicate touch. Then he tosses the rag onto the floor and backs away as he tucks his dick back into his pants. I'm left reeling, seated on the counter with my skirt around my waist, still quivering from that shock.

"Your pussy feels good, just like I thought it might."

I want to tell him how massive his cock is but I get the feeling he knows already. Instead, I slide off the counter onto unsteady feet and lean on his large frame. "Keep me safe, Sven," I mutter, not really knowing what I'm saying. I just don't want to run anymore.

"I will. If you marry me." Sven rights me, making sure I am standing before yanking my skirt back down. I laugh. I laugh so hard and so loud I might even wake Rico up, and Sven slaps a hand over my mouth. "It's not a joke," he says sternly and I calm myself.

"What?" I blink my eyes, seeing double now. Sven's face fades in and out of vision, blurring and then focusing. He takes my hand and opens the door, leading me to the couch where I collapse. He puts a pillow under my head, and covers me with the afghan that lays over the back of the sofa.

"Think about it." He jams his shirt back into the waistband of his pants and moves toward the door.

"Marry you? But I hardly know you," I slur, already feeling sleep pulling me in.

"You want to be safe don't you?" I hear the door lock click open and the squeak of the hinges. "I said think about it. Someone will be watching your place tonight. You'll be safe. Just sleep."

The door clicks shut and I lay there thinking about what he said. Marry him in exchange for safety? But, is that safe?

I am too drunk to really think rationally about this, but one thing I know for sure now. I can't leave in the morning. Not until I know what Sven really meant by that.

6

SVEN

The afternoon is warm, the sun beating down over my backyard. I sit near the pool in one of the deck chairs I had imported from Italy next to my brother Dominic. He is wearing a suit, like always, but I'm enjoying the weather in my shorts and t-shirt. This isn't a friendly call. It usually isn't when it comes to Dom. He's got too many things weighing on his shoulders to make house calls for socialization. Everything serves its purpose in this family—one of the reasons I'd rather not be named the next Pakhan. Dominic can have that title for all I care.

"Cigar?" I ask, reaching into my humidor. The Cubans smell fantastic, and they smoke even better. Dominic waves me off, which sours the mood. I shut the humidor with the intention to smoke when he leaves, and I fold my arms over my chest, reclined in the deck chair. He sits straighter, leaning forward on his knees.

"The sting with this Albanian guy who's got eyes on Red... how's that going?" His questions are direct, always. He loosens his tie and uses his handkerchief to mop sweat off his forehead. There is very little breeze in the city anyway, but in my tiny backyard with a seven-foot-tall privacy fence, it's reduced to nothing. That's why I put the pool in.

"I'm on it, Dom. You can trust me to finish my job. Just worry about the mole we have snooping around. I sent Red after some snooper last week. Bastard was prowling around the bookstore."

"Yeah, he told me." Dominic puts his handkerchief back into the breast pocket of his suit coat and slides the coat off his shoulders. Sweat rings hug his sides as he drapes the jacket over his knee. "Jimmy is working for me, Sven. I told you I have some business with searching for this mole that you don't know anything about. You keep your hands and Matty's off of him. Anyone else who knows too. Got it?" Dominic eyes me sternly and I know he's serious. The family business comes first, which means if I double cross him there will be hell to pay. Even my own father wouldn't bat an eyelash at putting lead in my skull if I am found to be helping the enemy.

"Yeah, I got it. But why not just use Red?" I reach for my bottled water and hand it to him. He seems to need it more than I do, though my skin is getting kissed by the sun and his is covered.

"Because do you think Red wants to put a bullet in Leo's skull if the mole turns out to be him?" Dom takes the water and unscrews the cap, gulping it down as if he is lost in a desert. He has a fair point. I wouldn't want to be the one to put my own brother down, and I wouldn't believe the evidence even if I see it with my own eyes. Which makes it a very clever plot indeed. I just pray that Leo isn't really part of this plot against Dominic and the family business.

"Fair enough." I cross my arms over my chest again and watch the water in the pool shake as the subway rumbles the ground below us.

Dominic concedes, pulling his tie off and unbuttoning the top few buttons of his shirt, then he rolls up his sleeves. Next he removes his shoes and socks and rests his bare toes on the pool deck. I knew the heat would get to him. I chuckle at his awkward appearance, but he doesn't pay attention to me. He continues on with his "meeting" as if nothing had happened.

"So the gun shipment got messed up. Leo and Nick are really messing things up down at the shipping yard. I trust Leo with my life, but I'm not sure Nick is the man for the job after all. Those guns were headed for Mexican territory and now we have a bounty on the head of every one of our guys because we didn't deliver. We need to smooth things out and get the shipment delivered now. This is up to you, Sven."

I don't have time to follow the Albanian around, track down a lost gun shipment that Leo dropped the ball on, and still track Allie. Hearing Dom add more to my plate than I'm desiring to do irritates me. I can't help but scowl and shake my head.

"You have a problem?" he asks, and I'm reminded that he is my boss, like it or not. When we were kids I used to kick the shit out of him. I'm twice as strong and three times as fast, but he's older and that's why he's in charge. I have always hated that. I don't want the responsibility, but I do want the respect, and he throws me trash jobs all the time, babysitting for someone else who should know better.

"Yeah, I have a problem. I have other things to do with my life than to follow Leo and Nick around cleaning up their piles of shit. I'm not animal control, you know." I stand, too frustrated to sit there next to him, and I pace the length of the pool. The deck is hot, threatening to burn my feet, but my anger drives me forward.

"Things like following that redhead around?" His question again is direct. He knows better than to play games with me anyway. I don't do riddles and I don't do manipulation.

"Yeah, just like that." I feel my jaw clenching of its own accord. I hate how he has my guys reporting to him on everything I do, just because I capped some loser in Central Park last year for spilling his coffee on my phone. He called me "out of control" and "irresponsible." What he didn't know at the time was the man was a major loser, had multiple counts of rape and a warrant out for his arrest. I did the city a favor.

"Tuck told me that you were following someone. Looks like the man she's with is dangerous too. He's got a rap sheet." Dominic walks over to the steps and dips his toes into the cool water. I can see how tempted he is to just climb in, but he probably has another meeting or two today. He's lucky I don't push him in just for being a twat to me.

"Yeah, I know what I'm doing. I'm forty-two, not twelve." I jam my hands into my pockets and join him, standing on the top step with my feet submerged. "Feels nice, right?"

"It does. But I don't have time for games, Sven. You take care of family first. That woman is not our concern." I see the hem of his slacks dipping into the water slightly and I snicker and shake my head.

"You shoulda worn shorts like I said. I told you it was hot today. Ninety degrees forecast means it feels like over a hundred." My comment draws a scowl and an eye roll from my older brother.

"Leave the woman alone. Focus on your priorities. You need to pay better attention to Leo and Nick. They need stronger supervision. Something is going down there and I want to know what it is."

Dominic retreats from the pool and picks up his tie, coat, and shoes. He leaves without any more to say, and I feel like the mood for a cigar is now ruined. Rex only did what he was ordered to do, and how can I blame him for being loyal to my brother over me? Dom is the next leader. To cross him would be to hang yourself.

I pick up my humidor and make my way back into the house, placing it on my desk. The day is halfway over and I have a bit of free time, so after calling Rex to find out how things are going with Allie, I make my way to the barber. Rex is watching over her today as she takes Rico to the park to play for a while with a friend. I'm surprised she didn't just try to jet after I saw all the boxes she has packed in her house. It looked to me like she was planning to leave the next morning, but it's been a week and she's still here. Rex would have followed her anyway, so I would know where she is at all times, but she hasn't tried to leave yet.

Given how sex with her went, I'd say she is sticking around because of me. That's a good thing. I don't want to have to chase her across the city. Having her only a few blocks from where I am at all times makes me feel more in control. Dominic is right too; I do have impulse control issues. Most of them can be mitigated with a bit of whiskey or a cigar to calm me down, but Allie is like the finest aged Scotch a man can buy. The idea of having her has given me a new focus I can't deny. Nothing has ever made me feel so alive or driven than the idea of claiming that beauty as my own.

The bell dings as I walk into the barber shop. My usual guy is deep into a cut with another person whom I don't recognize, so he seats me at a chair in the back, around the corner. "I'll be right with you, Sven. Just have to finish up here."

I relax back into the seat and listen to the soft music playing. Some loud laughter around the corner in the main part of the shop catches my attention. I hear the door ring again, someone coming or going. It isn't often I have to wait for my barber to get to me, but I did just walk in without an appointment. So I try to remain calm. I turn the chair slowly, taking in the sight of this side of the shop. I'm normally in the front.

The door to the office is open. I can see Lenny's jacket hanging on the back of his chair. There are three other stations back here, all of them empty, and all of them perfectly cleaned and organized, ready for their next customer to receive a haircut or shave. They all have a reclining chair, sink, counter with all the necessary tools, and a mirror. I catch a glimpse of my reflection in one as my eyes sweep across them, then I see from my angle the rest of the shop.

My guy—Carry—is dusting hair off the shoulders of another gentleman. Lenny is working on someone whose face I cannot see, obstructed by his body. The man's reflection in the mirror behind him only shows the back of his head, but I hear his voice. He's loud and arrogant, talking about some mishap.

"Yeah, so he should have met his maker the other day but he gave us the slip. Somehow, he was tipped off."

"That fucker is going down, you know?" A second man, whom I cannot see at all, speaks with just as much arrogance. I'm in the business of knowing who is doing what in this city, and these idiots are deep in Russian territory. They have to know we have eyes and ears everywhere.

"Well, when we nab the girl he's going to come hunting, and when he does, we will get him." The first man seems confident that whoever they're hunting for is meeting their end, which makes me curious. I crane my neck but I still can't manage to see either of their faces. And not wanting to draw attention to myself, I try to relax.

"Dom is not as stupid as you think he is. You're putting your life in jeopardy."

My chest constricts. I hear my brother's name on their lips and it makes me want to go slit their throats. I pull my phone out of my pocket, ready to call Dominic instantly, but instead I have a good idea. I call Lenny's office number, knowing he will go back to answer the call and move out of the way. I'll get a good look at the man's face that way. The minute I hit send and the phone rings, Lenny glances at his office. My plan is working.

I prepare myself as Lenny moves toward me, trying to maneuver my body so I can see around him, but he looms larger the closer he comes, and blocks my view even more. When I hear the bell at the door ding, I know someone has either left the shop or entered, and I stand abruptly, hoping to see the man Lenny was working on.

The chair is empty, the culprits gone. Lenny closes in and I grab his arm. "Hey, Sven, what's going on? I gotta get my phone."

I end the call on my phone and the ringing ceases. He glances at my hand and then looks with fear into my eyes. "What is it?"

"Who was that man?" I ask, nodding to the empty chair where the guy was just seated.

"I swear I don't know, Sven. He just walked in off the street. I never seen him before in my life." Lenny holds his hands up innocently. He knows who I am and what I will do to him if he's lying, so I trust him. Why wouldn't I? Lenny has no stake in this game. He won't care if he's giving his money to Dominic or me; money is money, and to own a shop on this block means he pays up.

"You swear to me you never seen him!" I am enraged now, probably too much so to sit for a haircut.

"Yeah, Sven, I swear." I hear the fear in his voice and I let go of him and back away. I should have jumped up and walked over to those guys the instant I heard them talking. I should have paid better attention to them as I walked past. These are the tiny details I used to pay attention to before I got distracted by Allie. Maybe Dominic is right. Maybe I am not focused enough on the things that are important. Maybe I have lost my touch because of a woman.

"Your cameras, do they work?"

"No, they are out because of that storm the other night. I'm sorry, Sven." He looks at me pleadingly but I have no intention of harming him.

I barge out of the shop and my hand goes straight to my phone. I dial the number for the office at the port, but instead of Leo, Nick picks up.

"Yo, this is Nick."

"Nick, we have a situation. Look, I can't get into details right now; I just need to know that the shipment is secure. We have to have those guns. We have people out here ready to kill Dominic over this shit and—"

"Woah, slow down. We got all that worked out now." Nick's nonchalant attitude irks me. He never takes things seriously and I don't understand how my father put him in this position. "Hey, Sven, you know Dominic wants these guns shipped to the Mexicans but I think we can turn a profit here. My guys tell me we can get almost four times the money for them in the city."

"The orders are to ship to the Mexicans. The LA streets need these things more than here and we already have a buyer." This isn't the first time Nick has tried to get me to go against Dominic's orders. A lot of what he says makes sense, and if I were Dominic I'd go about things a different way.

"But a million is so much more money than two-hundred-fifty. Don't you think? I mean imagine the pride on your father's face when you turn that profit for the family." Nick is persuasive but I can't defy Dominic. Not if I want him on my side when it comes to Allie.

"Just ship them. You make a great argument, but orders are orders. As long as Dominic is the boss, I have to do what he says. I expect the payment in the account tomorrow." I hang up, realizing I am in the wrong business. I need to take a step back from this shit and reevaluate what I want out of my life. Because right now what I want is Allie, not gun shipments or money. It's obvious that is where my focus is, because I'm screwing things up and there is nothing I can do about it. Not until she is mine.

7

ALLIE

My eye doesn't leave Rico for a second. He swings alongside a few girls around his same age while Sarah and I sit on a bench no more than twenty yards away. It's a great day for the park, but my nerves are high. I don't usually risk taking Rico in public, but Sven assured me the last time we spoke that he has men watching us—Rico specifically. He knows how strongly I feel about Rico staying safe, and the fact that I haven't left town yet must speak volumes to him. He got in my head and now I don't want to leave. I want to see where this goes.

"So tell me, then, if this guy Paul is scaring you so badly, what keeps you here? You've been all over this city, babe. I know you. You don't stick around when your ex comes. You bolt." Sarah sips an iced coffee through a straw while badgering me. She's been hounding me the past three days about Sven and what happened after she left the house that night. She's seen the boxes piled around my living room and knows me better than to believe my procrastination is solely based on money.

I shrug, hiding a smirk. "I have my reasons." Sven is the only reason, though I'm not even sure if he's a good reason. Great sex isn't the same as a man who will cherish and protect me, though he has done the latter. I'm just not sure he's the "cherish" type. Sven is rough around the edges, impulsive and a bit demanding.

"It's that beast of a man, isn't it?" she jokes, jabbing me in the ribs. I snicker and look at her, taking my eyes off of Rico as a few boys run past with remote control cars in hand. Their laughter puts me at ease. With so many people in this park I don't see how Paul would ever make a move today. I glance at Rico, still on the swings, and settle in for the conversation. I don't see Sven's men, but that doesn't mean they're not here.

"Okay, so you need to hear this," I tell her, leaning in. I let my guard down, knowing Rico is there but believing he will be fine on the swings while Sarah and I chat. She leans into me too, straw pinched between her lips, slurping cold coffee. "He thinks he can protect me from Paul..." I let the words hover, unsure if I should tell her about exactly what he wants in exchange.

"And? Is that a bad thing? You could stay where you are, not have to move. And Rico loves Henry, that little boy downstairs. He's actually made friends this time." Sarah frowns. I know she loves him like her own, and my heart feels the same way hers does. I don't want to uproot Rico anymore. Part of me believes that if we just left the state Paul would never know where we went, but I feel like I'd have fewer job opportunities and I'd miss my friends too.

"But there's a catch," I say, glancing at Rico. For a moment I don't see him, but my eye catches a flash of red—the color of his shirt—as he ascends the stairs to the jungle gym equipment. He is racing a young girl to the top. I turn back to Sarah just as she clears her throat.

"What's that? It costs something? Pay it girl. You need a bodyguard." She shakes her head and leans back on her seat. The way she sits with such confidence baffles me. I've been beaten down too many times to fully have that same confidence. I live in fear, so I understand her desire to protect me; I'm just not sure Sven's request is the right price for my life.

"He wants me to marry him," I blurt out, no longer feeling like I should hold back. Sarah is my best friend; if anyone can talk me out of this insanity it's her.

"Wait, what?" she says, nearly spitting a mouthful of iced frappe out. A few drops dribble down her chin and she wipes them away as her eyes grow wide with shock. "You're joking, right?"

"No, I'm not. And neither was he. He told me he would protect me from Paul, but only if I married him. It's insane, right? Am I just a little stupid for even considering it?" I run a hand through my hair. My forehead is damp with sweat, so are my palms. It's a hot day, but the topic of Sven and his stern proposal give me anxiety. I like him, but we have talked less than five times. And the sex was amazing, but that does not constitute a relationship.

"Wow, he's crazy. He really said that?" She gawks at me while I nod my head then she continues. "I mean, divorce is a thing." I see her wheels turning, her eyes looking upward toward the cloudless evening sky as she purses her lips. "This guy is loaded, Allie. You could marry him. Take advantage of the great sex, his money, and the safety, and when Paul is gone for good, you just divorce him. You could have a huge payout." She laughs so hard she snorts, but I don't see the humor in it. I can't toy with someone's emotions.

"Yeah, I just don't see that happening. He's a pretty serious guy. And how could I ever lead him on and let him think I was actually interested in him when my entire plan was to divorce him and hurt him?" I shake my head, turning away from her to find Rico. My eyes scan the entire playground, searching for a hint of his red shirt. Another boy with a red shirt runs past, but his hair is blond, not the warm auburn tones of Rico's hair.

I look to where the swings are, but he's not there. Then I scan the equipment, waiting until a few kids go down the slide to make sure he isn't just held up in the giant plastic tube. I don't see him anywhere and my heart starts to beat fast.

"Uh, Sarah, do you see Rico?" I ask, standing. I hear her mumble something but it's not coherent. I move toward the playground, certain in my own head that as soon as I get closer he will emerge from a hiding spot I've not yet thought of, but dread begins to weigh down every step. "Rico!" I call, cupping my mouth. A few children look in my direction but I still don't see him. "Sarah!"

Sarah is at my side in an instant, clasping my arm to her chest. "I don't see him, Allie." Her voice sounds frantic, the way my heart feels. I weave through the children with their moms at their sides. Women are staring at me, glancing around the park too.

"Rico! This isn't funny. Come out!" I spin around in a circle, thinking I've just missed him. I've walked past him and that's it. It's a simple explanation for why I don't see him. But I look in every corner of the playground and he's not here.

"Look, he was with that girl!" Sarah hisses, pointing, and I see the young redhead who was running around with Rico moments ago. I run over to her, tears already brimming in my eyes. She looks frightened as I drop to my knees next to her and grab her hand.

"Honey, where did Rico go?"

"Who's Rico?" she asks, scrunching her nose. A woman dressed in bright purple approaches me, looking concerned. I address my next comment to her.

"Ma'am, is this your daughter? She was playing with my son. I can't find him. Did you see him? Did you see which way he went?"

The woman's face softens as she pulls her little girl into her arms, the girl clearly frightened now. She shakes her head. "I did just see him. Dark hair, red shirt?" I nod and she continues. "He was just here. They were going on the slide." Her frown only makes my heart panic more.

"Rico!" I scream, bolting to my feet. My mind is racing as I begin to tear across the park, looking behind trees and trash cans. In moments I hear sirens, though I didn't call the cops. Sarah must have had the forethought to do so, because in my panicked state, I can't even see straight let alone think of proper steps. He is gone. There is no trace of him.

I drop to my knees, a mess of anxiety and terror, and a police officer approaches me. He crouches next to me and offers his hand. "Ma'am, I'm Officer Tiney, here to help you. I understand your son went missing. We need a solid description of him. Where was he? What is he wearing? Do you have a photo?"

I rub my eyes and think. I don't even have my wallet with me. No picture of him, and my brain isn't functioning. I throw up, dousing the grass with a hefty pile of spaghetti, which was formerly my dinner. The officer walks away, returning with Sarah to comfort me. She helps me to my feet and puts an arm around me.

"We're going to find him, Al. I told the cops everything. I showed them a photo from my phone from the other day when I babysat." She guides me toward the benches where we were just seated and I sob hysterically.

"Paul… he took him. I know it." Covering my mouth, I collapse onto the bench and curl into a ball, hugging my knees. "Paul did this. He's got my boy."

"Shhh, you don't know that." Sarah's hand smooths down my back and around in circles. "Look, we're going to find him. Maybe he just went to the toilets."

I only cry harder. I don't even know how much time passes as I sit on the bench with cops asking me a dozen questions each, but the sun goes down, and it's dark. Central park is terrifying to children in the dark, and I can't imagine Rico out there all alone.

When a figure shrouded in shadow approaches, I feel my hope rising. Before he even gets to me I stand and run to him. Sven's chest is hard as a rock as I bury my face in it, wrapping my arms around him. He holds me to himself and I hear him wave Sarah off with a few words. Then I hear one of the cops talking to him.

"I'll bring her home. And Jim, tell the gang I have this. Make it look good. Give Danny the credit or something." Sven's voice rumbles in his chest, vibrating my cheek, but I don't let go. "Can you walk?" he asks me, but I'm in a daze still. When I don't answer he picks me up and carries me.

"Sven, Paul took him." I'm a blubbering fool as I cling to this man I hardly know. Why am I clinging to him? Why has this shut me down so much that I can't even aid the police in the search? Why does Paul scare me like this?

"No, he didn't." Sven's voice is stern, the way I remember. I look up into his eyes as he sets me on the ground. We are near a large black SUV, the door standing open. "Get in," he says with authority and I don't hesitate. I climb into the back seat of the car and see Rico seated there playing a handheld video game. He looks up at me with a sulking expression and rolls his eyes.

"Oh my god, baby," I gasp, pulling him onto my lap. He squirms to get away.

"I wanted to go with Dad. This jerk told me to get in his car." He scowls and huffs out a sigh. "At least he has a Gameboy." Video game still in hand, Rico pushes off my lap and sits next to me and I turn to Sven, who climbs in next to me. There are two more men seated in the front seats, and Sven shuts the door, closing me and Rico in with him.

"The man did try to take the boy, ma'am, but we stopped him and had a nice friendly chat." The driver adjusts the rearview mirror and looks back at me in the reflection. "He has a new piercing, if you know what I mean."

As the man says that, Sven opens his jacket and flashes his weapon so I can see it. I cover my mouth and gasp. "You shot him?" I hiss under my breath, not knowing if Rico can hear me. Sven raises his eyebrows and sighs.

"Your son is safe. The man in question walked away—or ran. It doesn't matter to me how fast he left."

My chest is so tight I'm finding it hard to breathe, but my Rico is safe. This was a very close call. Paul could have been in the next state with my boy already and I'd never see him again. It was time for me to take this more seriously. I should have left town when I had the chance, but my stupid emotions and my damn sex drive just kept me here confused. I need to protect Rico at all costs.

"My offer stands," Sven says, reaching into his pocket. He pulls out a ring and holds it up in front of my face, pinched between thumb and finger. Part of me wonders if Paul was even here, or if Sven's men took Rico just to make me afraid Paul would do such a thing. But Rico wouldn't lie. He said he wanted to be with his dad and these men stopped that. My heart sinks as I realize how close I came to losing him.

"I'll take the offer." I say the words without another thought. If marrying Sven is what keeps Rico away from Paul, then I have no other choice. Paul will always chase me down. He will always find me, always come for Rico. "Divorce is always an option," I mumble under my breath.

"We won't need that. You'll see." Sven's confidence is comforting, but what I need now isn't comfort; it's safety. "I can take you to your place to get whatever things you want. You will move in with me tonight."

As he speaks, Rico's eyes pop up, but only for a second. He is absorbed in his video game again in seconds and completely unaware that his entire life is about to change again. Only this time, it will be more than just where he lives. I swallow a growing lump and sink deeper into the leather bench seat of the SUV. What the hell am I agreeing to?

8

SVEN

I stand near the door, waiting as Allie puts some things in a bag. A few of the boxes that were stacked up along the wall the last time I was here are now sitting in different places, open with some of their contents hanging out. The evidence that she is planning to leave is everywhere. I am confident with this new arrangement that her need to run from that jerk is gone.

"But, Mom, Jordan is here." Rico sits on the sofa with his spindly arms crossed over his chest defiantly. "I don't want to move again." His dark hair and eyes remind me of his father, which is not a good thing, but I try to separate my feelings for that creep from this moment.

"I know, bud, but it isn't safe here anymore. Okay? Sven is going to help us out and we will stay with him now. I don't think we will have to move again for a while." Allie's tone tells me she's sad about this move too, but I don't know whether it is only because her son is hurting or if she is also regretting the decision to marry me. My arrangement might not be normal, but when I see a good thing, I just take it.

"We should go soon," I say firmly, reminding her that I am waiting. She glances at me, and I see hesitation in her gaze. "I can send someone for any belongings you want later on."

Rico pouts at her, brow furrowed every time he looks at me. I'm an intrusion into his life that he doesn't seem to want at all. He'll learn, just like her, that I am the best thing that has ever happened to them. Their life just got elevated several levels.

"Mom, please?" Rico's whining is louder this time, complete with a dramatic head loll. My father would have smacked me around a bit, but Allie is patient, patting his head.

"It's for the best, baby. Okay?" Allie glances at me again, more fear in her eyes. "Let's go."

"No! I don't want to." Rico throws himself back on the sofa and shouts his displeasure, but Allie is so calming. She reminds me of my own mother. She sits next to him and pulls him onto her lap.

"Look, I will make sure you get to play with Jordan, okay?" She talks to him in a calm tone. "This time is the last time. I give you my word."

After several minutes of cajoling, Rico is on his feet, carrying his bag to the waiting car. Allie only brings one bag with her, the rest will be sent for. I lead them to the SUV and we load up then head out. Matty drives; he and Rex have been by my side all evening. If not for them, Paul would have a bullet in his head, not his shoulder. And Rico would have seen the whole thing instead of being whisked away to safety while I dealt with things.

We pull up in front of my sprawling home and Allie's jaw drops. She cranes her neck to see out the window, looking up at the three-story-tall Victorian. I have spent hundreds of thousands of dollars reno-vating it and restoring it to its natural beauty. Some men of my stature would be pleased to have the newest furnishings and most contemporary designs. I'm much more in tune with history and the aesthetic of class and sophistication, even when it comes at a cost.

"Woah, Sven. Your place is huge." Rico clicks his tongue as he slides out of the car toting his bag on his shoulder. "Do you got any video games?" he asks, staring up at me with large eyes. I nod at him.

"I have just about any system you want in my gaming room. If you'd like, I can just have your bed put in there. It can be your bedroom." I hold the door as Allie climbs out. Her jaw is still slack as she takes in her surroundings. The block my home sits on is one historic home after another, crammed together like sardines in a can, but mine stands out. I like it that way.

"I think that's not a great idea," she mumbles as she gets her bearings. Her eyes meet mine in a firm gaze and I see a stubborn side of her. I like it. She'll be fun to break.

"Let's get off the street." I gesture at the front door and Rico races up the steps. When I let us into the foyer, the amazement continues. It's refreshing to see someone so enamored of the hard work I've put into this place. I've gotten so used to it I pass by with hardly an ounce of attention paid.

"Where are the games?" Rico asks, turning abruptly to face me. I'm happy he is no longer throwing a fit. Allie glowers at him but I point up the steps.

"Second floor, third room on the right. You'll probably meet Odin. He's around somewhere."

"Odin?" Allie asks, eyebrows high.

"German shepherd. He's nice, don't worry."

"Oh cool, a dog too!" Rico celebrates, clapping his hands, and then races up the steps, leaving his bag sit on the ground next to the door. I will have to get used to having a child in the house. And I'll have to let Marta know we have new occupants. She'll have to cook more often and probably clean a lot more—at least with a young boy to watch after.

"Well, I'd say Rico will adjust just fine." I turn to Allie who is glaring at me.

"We are not putting his bed in the game room. He is a child. He needs discipline and—"

"I'm not going to tell you how to parent your child." I clear my throat and wait for her angry glare to resolve. "I have a game room for myself because I enjoy a good game now and then. He is welcome to use it when you please. I thought maybe he'd feel more comfortable this evening after the incident if he were surrounded by things to distract himself."

Her expression softens further and she nods. "Thank you," she said, and I get the feeling she is eating words she hasn't yet spoken.

"I'm not a maniac, Allie." I nod at the open door to our left and say, "My den..." I brush past her, walking into my den, and she follows. "You can leave your things sit by the door. Gerard will bring it to my room."

I continue on toward the liquor cabinet but I sense Allie hovering near the door. When I glance over my shoulder she is glued to the floor just inside the den. She looks like a deer caught in headlights, eyes wide, chest heaving. Certainly she didn't think she would be getting her own room when she came here to be my wife.

"Come in," I order, and she looks at the floor near the door, then sets her bag down. As she creeps closer I pour a glass of whiskey for each of us, then hand it to her when she finally meets me in the center of the large room beneath the chandelier.

"You have a butler?" she asks, taking the glass.

"And a maid." I sip my whiskey and move to one of the leather couches, sitting down. Allie follows timidly, clutching the glass of whiskey.

"Are they like slaves?" Her voice quavers as she speaks.

I chuckle. "Do you think I'm a monster or something? I pay my staff well. They are free to find a new job any time they want. They enjoy working for me because the job comes with benefits." I eye her over the rim of my glass as I take another sip.

She nods and squirms, looking a little more relaxed. This game of cat and mouse is interesting. If anyone is uncomfortable here, it isn't my staff. Allie's regrets shine through the feigned calm she exudes like sunlight through a sheer curtain. She takes tiny sips of her whiskey, her eyes absorbing every detail of the room, from the Persian rug on the floor to the textured ceiling overhead.

"You act like you've never seen the home of a wealthy person." My glass is empty, so I stand and retrieve the bottle, bringing it back to top off my glass and hers. She tries to resist, but I have my reasons for pouring her another round.

"I, uh... I honestly haven't. My parents were quite poor, barely made ends meet. Paul, well he had more money, but he put it all up his nose or drank it away." Allie looks down into her drink. "Being a single mom is rough." Her shoulders droop.

"Well, you'll never have to worry about money again. I have plenty of it to go around. I don't want you working that job anymore either. It's too dangerous for you to be out and about. Once your ex—"

"Quit my job?" She looks upset with me, shifting away from me on the couch. "I don't think so."

"What do you need a job for when I will provide everything you could ever need?"

She clears her throat and downs the entire drink aggressively. When she sets the glass on the glass top table a little harder than I'd like, I can tell she's not pleased with my desires. "First of all, I'm independent, and I'd like to continue being that way. Also, I prefer to keep my job so I can have contact with the outside world, you know—make friends."

She crosses her arms over her chest in a cute protest that doesn't move me at all, except to make me want to bend her over the couch and fuck the daylights out of her. I've always loved to play hard to get and this one might just be my match.

"We'll discuss it later I suppose. For now, you can just adjust to having a few days off and think about how you'd like to respond to your future husband from now on." I keep my eyes trained on her as she scoffs, eyebrows high, and sucks in a breath to say something. She doesn't say a word, though, her shoulders dropping in defeat again.

"You know I don't know if I even like you as a person. The only reason I agreed to this scheme is because I need your protection to keep Paul away from Rico. That scared the shit out of me." She rubs her arms, hugging herself. She doesn't have to tell me how she feels because I can read her like a book, but I appreciate her honesty. It puts us on the same page so I know what I'm working with.

I lean forward, elbows on knees, and clasp my glass in both hands. "Arranged marriages happen all the time, and they turn out really great for some people. You'll see that this whole thing is fate playing in your favor."

Allie sighs and her eyes flick toward the door where Gerard has already come and gone silently. Her bag is probably in my room now, waiting for her to unpack her things. Her inability to relax in my presence amuses me. In time she'll learn she has nothing to fear from me at all and that she can trust my decisions for her. Until then we'll have this awkward tension, mostly because she reacts awkwardly to me.

"May I go to my room now? I would like to lie down. The whiskey made me a bit tired. And where is it? Can you show me? Maybe I can say goodnight to Rico before I lay down." She stands uncomfortably, arms still hugging her middle.

"Well as a future husband to you I expect some sort of reciprocity. It's only natural that certain behaviors that happen between partners would happen in this relationship too." My eyes stay trained on her over the rim of my glass as I finish the drink, then set it on the table next to hers. Her eyes narrow and her brow furrows.

"Behaviors? Reciprocity?"

"Yes, Allie. I'm going to be your husband. Certain conjugal duties that a wife has for her husband should be in effect. Don't you think?"

"Ugh..." she scoffs, backing away a step. "You want sex?"

I stand and slip out of my jacket, draping it over the back of the couch before rolling up my sleeves. "It's only fair. You're being provided with a place to stay, round the clock protection, and let's not forget how I saved Rico tonight. He could be halfway to Maine in the back of his father's car."

Her face falls. She looks pale, glancing at the door again. Then she turns back to me biting her lip.

"You didn't like the sex last week?" I advance on her, loosening my belt as I walk. She doesn't back away.

"No, I did," she says, protesting still. "I just..."

"You just thought you'd get a free ride? No obligation on your end? What does 'marry me' mean to you?" I pull my belt free of the belt buckles and fold it in half, gripping both ends in one hand. She blinks several times, looking down at the belt then back up at my face.

"I just thought... We hardly know each other and I..." She licks her lips.

"So you like the sex, you want my protection, you're not sure if you like me, but you'll marry me. You just don't want to have sex with me? Not even if I make your toes curl in a pantie dropping way?"

She licks her lips again. I can tell she's thinking about it. What's not to enjoy? I don't understand her hesitation. I walk into her bubble and she tenses, shoulders drawing up. Her knuckles turn white, hands clenched into fists.

"I'm not going to hurt you, Allie, but I am going to take what is rightfully mine. My wife will submit to me and please me sexually. There is no reason we can't start tonight." I wrap an arm around her waist and pull her stiff body into me. She whimpers and backs up, but I hold her against myself. "Would you like another glass of whiskey first? Help you loosen up?"

"If I say no, you will stop. Right?" Her voice shakes as she speaks. It's cute.

"Of course. I'm not a barbarian, and I'm not a monster. I want sex from my beautiful bride to be. That's all."

She softens at the compliment and I know somewhere deep inside her is a naughty little minx waiting to come out and play. I saw her the other night in her bathroom, and that is the Allie I want.

"So, drink or no?" I ask again, and she bites her lip and nods her head.

"Please. I need it…"

Three glasses of whiskey is all it takes to get her to consent? This is going to be easier than I thought.

9

ALLIE

The whiskey makes my head swim, but I down the third drink as quickly as I can. I want it to saturate every cell in my being. It's not that I don't want Sven—I do, more than he will ever know. It's the matter of principle, that sex between two people should be born of a deep desire and attraction, not out of obligation. I set the glass down on his table and turn to see him shirtless, sliding his slacks down. His shoes are already neatly tucked under the edge of the table.

"Take your clothes off, Allie," he orders, laying his belt over the arm of the couch. I wonder what he's got planned with that.

I hesitate, looking away from his gaze. I'm not sure if I want to go through with this, but it's too late to back down now. I slowly pull my t-shirt off over my head and reach behind my back to unhook my bra, letting it slide down my arms and onto the floor. I can feel his eyes on me, burning into my skin.

He takes a step closer, his hand reaching out to cup my breast. I flinch at his touch, but he doesn't seem to notice. He squeezes gently, causing a moan to escape my lips. He traces his thumb over my nipple, watching as it hardens under his touch.

I reach down to unbutton my jeans, trying to ignore the heavy feeling in my stomach. As I slide them down my legs, he moves in closer, his breath hot against my ear.

"Good girl," he whispers, his hands running over my bare skin. I can feel his hardness pressing against my thigh, and I know what's coming next. I feel myself beginning to sway as I stand up, the alcohol making it difficult to keep my balance. My eyes are locked on Sven as he leans against me, his body rippling with muscle. It's hard to resist him when he's like this, all commanding and powerful. His eyes rake over my body hungrily, and I can see the desire burning in his gaze.

"You're mine tonight, Allie," he growls, his lips crashing down on mine in a fierce kiss. I can feel his hands on my body, rough and possessive, as he pushes me up against the wall.

I'm not sure if I'm ready for this, but it's too late now. I close my eyes and surrender to his touch, my body trembling with anticipation. I can feel his arousal growing as I wrap my arms around his neck, my desire for him coursing through my veins. I don't know what's going to happen next.

The alcohol has drained my inhibitions, and his hungry, grazing hands have begun to push my buttons. The kiss grows hotter, his tongue searching my mouth as he backs me across the room. I hear the clink of his belt buckle and know he's picked it up, but with my eyes shut and my arms draped around his neck, I care more about the growing ache in my groin.

"God... you need to make me come," I pant against his mouth. He growls in response and my backside slams into something firm—his desk. I whimper as his lips pull away from mine, and I open my eyes to see his hungry gaze as he plunges two fingers between my legs, searching for my entrance.

"You're going to milk my dick until I fill you with my seed." My eyes widen as he says the words, and I feel my cheeks flush with embarrassment. I can't believe he said that, but at the same time, I can't help but feel a thrill of excitement run through my veins.

I nod in response, my body trembling with anticipation as he pushes his fingers deep inside of me. He knows just how to move them, how to push me closer and closer to the edge. I can feel my orgasm building and my breath coming in shallow gasps.

"Come for me, Allie," he orders, his voice thick with desire. I let out a loud cry as I come, my body shaking with pleasure as he pumps his fingers in and out of me. He pulls them out and I hear his belt buckle clink again. "Good girl," he says, biting the top of my shoulder roughly. "Now bend over."

Sven forces me to turn around and pushes me down across his desk. He is strong, manhandling me and forcing me to submit. After that orgasm, how can I not? I whimper as my cheek presses down on the cool wood of his desk, my breasts crushed beneath me. His cock prods at my backside, sliding in and out of my juices until he finds my hole.

"God..." I moan as he pushes into me, his length filling me up completely. "Fuck, you're huge," I moan, gripping the edge of the desk with one hand. It feels like he'll tear me.

"Your tight little pussy needs to loosen up a bit to take all of me," he says, and I wonder how much more of him there is. He's already so deep it feels like he'll enter my womb, so I don't even want to ask. I can't even if I wanted to—he's fucking me so hard I can't breathe.

"Shit... oh shit," I moan, and then the belt buckle clinks again.

I don't even have time to react. The leather makes contact with my ass, smacking me hard. I yelp, but the pain is strangely erotic, pushing my arousal to the next level, especially when he growls in pleasure. He keeps spanking me, alternating between hard and gentle strokes until

I'm moaning and begging him to stop. I can barely take it anymore, but he doesn't stop.

He smacks me again, pushing against my entrance as he does. I can't believe how good it feels, and I cry out louder with each smack, my body trembling with pleasure. I'm so close to the edge again and I can feel him right there with me.

"Fuck, you're hot," he grunts and my pussy clenches around him gripping him like a vice. I let out a loud cry as my orgasm crashes through me, his length pushing me over the edge. He follows soon after, his body shaking as he pumps his seed into me. It's hot, warming my insides, then draining down my inner thigh.

I hear the belt drop, then feel his fingers at my entrance as he pulls out. He smears my juices around, mixing them with what drains out of me from him. "God, your pussy is so amazing, so tight still. I can't wait to stretch that thing so it can take my full length."

I shudder as I stand up. More of him drains out of me and I grimace at the mess. My legs are weak and wobbly. There is no box of tissues, no handkerchief. Nothing to wipe myself clean, except the clothing I want to put back on. His sex is incredible, but I don't feel comfortable being naked and alone with him yet.

"Do you have a tissue so I can clean myself?" I ask, feeling timid. The alcohol is starting to wane slightly. I want another drink. Sven seems to know already, and he pours me a glass. His dick, still mostly hard, stands up proud like a peacock. He's not ashamed to be naked in front of me, but my arms across my chest make me feel more comfortable.

"Here," he says, thrusting the glass into my hand. I take it, drinking it down eagerly as he walks across the room. He picks up his slacks and boxers, then something else. He dresses as I finish the drink then set my glass on the desk behind me. As he returns to me, he dangles my panties from one finger.

"I need to wipe myself clean. Your cum is on my leg."

855

"Nah...I like it that way." Sven offers a sinister grin as he wads my panties up and reaches between my legs. It's shocking to me that he's so bold, and I have no time to react as he starts shoving the lacy material inside of me. I plant both hands firmly on the desk and lock eyes with him until the material is gone, and his fingers are teasing my clit. "That should stimy the flow," he says, winking.

I am so turned on by him again that I know I could come again right now if he wanted to fuck me again. But I bite my tongue. This arrangement with him will be mutually beneficial, even if I get more out of the deal than him. I take a deep breath and he backs away, taking my glass to fill it again.

I'm tired, ready to lie down, but I have no clue where my bed is—or his bed. It appears I will be sleeping with him. The butler took my bag when I wasn't looking, and I don't know if anyone is around to show me to my room, so I hover near his desk, waiting for him to fill my drink. He does, then returns to my side with what I know will be the drink that has me passing out.

"Thank you," I tell him.

"For the orgasms or the alcohol?"

Sven is a puzzle to me. I'm not sure how to take his comments sometimes. I want to think he is noble and good, but there is a mystery about him that makes me think he is harboring some dark secret, maybe worse than Paul.

"For both," I say, and I mean it.

He walks away from me, toward the sofa, and I turn and look at the books on the book shelves. Scattered amongst the books are pictures in frames, tchotchkes of all kinds, and old pieces of art. My eye catches on a particular photo of what appears to be Sven with an older man, his father maybe. I remember the face from the television. A news report indicating this man—whoever he is—was ailing and getting worse by the day. I can't remember if the news report said why he is important enough to be noted on television, but I will never forget the face.

"This is your dad?" I ask, sipping the alcohol. I stand there staring at the photo. The more I study it the easier it is to see that the two men in the framed image are related. Same face, same eyes. I hear movement and then sense Sven standing behind me. His body heat radiates outward, kissing my bare skin.

"It is," he says.

I glance downward and behind myself. His hand is inches from my skin. It tingles my nerves, making goosebumps appear. His proximity has me wanting him again. The brush of the material inside me just barely fluttering over my entrance is arousing. He seems to sense that I like him there too, moving closer to me.

"He seems like a good man," I mutter absently, then reach for his hand. This man could make me come ten times and I would beg for more every time. I guide his hand to my mound, pressing his fingers against my clit, and he takes over, massaging my sensitive nub as he grinds his groin against me. He's still slightly hard.

"Oh god…" I moan, letting my head fall back against his shoulder. The whiskey is in full control now. Sober Allie would never do this.

"You like that? You want to come again?" he asks, nibbling on my neck. It makes my nipples harden and stand erect.

"Shit, Sven… I want your dick in me." I grab his wrist with one hand, feeling the whiskey slosh out of the cup onto my fingers in my other hand.

"Want me to lick you clean first? Taste that mess you made?" His breath is hot, making my groin ache again.

I don't get to answer because we're rudely interrupted. A bang at the front door, followed by the shuffling of footsteps has Sven pulling away and me reeling around to see a man covered in blood, eyes wide. He staggers into the room and Sven huffs out a sigh.

"Shit, boss, I'm sorry. I didn't know..." He collapses on the couch clutching his side.

I have no clue what to say or do. Sven goes into action, moving straight for his suit coat where he pulls out a handkerchief and tosses it at the man. "Hold it on the wound. I'll call Manning." Sven searches the floor where his clothing lay previously and picks up his phone. "Allie, out," he orders.

"What but I'm naked," I protest, covering my breasts as the bleeding man watches my every move.

"Get the fuck out," he orders again, pointing at the door.

I scurry over and reach for my clothing, but the man has his giant bloody boot on my things. I whimper and look up at Sven, mortified that this stranger is seeing me drunk, naked, and dripping with another man's cum.

"Out!" he screams and feeling tears welling up, I rush into the hallway. It's dark, and I'm scared. If Rico comes out and sees me naked, I will have no way to explain what's going on. I shrink back against the wall, hearing Sven's baritone voice booming behind the door which he slams shut. I stand there for a few minutes, crying softly and wondering what hell I've just walked into of my own accord.

And a woman walks up, carrying a blanket. She wraps it around my shoulders and gestures for me to follow her, so I do.

"Here, dear, you come with me," she coos, and I'm helpless without her. I follow her down a long dark hallway and she opens a door, flicking the lights on.

"You're the maid?" I ask, trembling as I follow her into the room.

"Yes, dear."

"Who was that man?" I clutch the blanket around my body and look around the room. My bag is sitting on the foot of the bed. I move toward it, sucked in by gravity.

"You need to shower and lie down now. He will come in here before too long." She smiles at me and moves toward a closed door within the room. When she opens it and turns on the light, I see that it's a bathroom. I hear water begin to run and she reemerges. "There. Now you clean up."

"But..."

"No buts," she whispers.

"Aren't you scared?" I hiss as she uses an arm around my waist to guide me to the bathroom. I sway on my feet as I walk. I'm ready to pass out now.

"I trust Sven with my life. You should too. Now, in the bath you go." The maid peels the blanket away from me and I stand exposed again. "In..." she urges.

I have no choice but to climb into the bath and sit down. It slowly fills as I sink into the warm water and I lay my head back. I'm so drunk, my eyes are heavy, so I let them flutter shut, and I vaguely remember the water turning off before I pass out. I have to get out of this place. It's not safe.

10

SVEN

"I t was that bastard Hensley." David grips his side where blood flows freely from a gunshot wound. He's staining my couch because of Allie's ex and this entire thing just got personal. I dial the number for Dr. Manning and wait for it to ring through.

"Sit tight, David. I'm calling for Manning now." I hold the phone to my ear as David recounts the story with jagged breaths. The way he sucks in air shows just how much pain he's in. Blood pours from his chest.

"We were just packing up her things. This bastard rushes in unannounced and starts shooting. I copped one to the side here, and Lenny nearly took one to the head. He was out for blood, Sven. If that woman was there, she'd be dead." David wheezes and I wonder if the bullet grazed his lungs.

"Alright, just rest." I pace the floor, hoping his blood doesn't drip on my Persian rug.

"Sven?" Manning answers the call and I step away from David to answer.

"Doc, we need you here, stat. David took a bullet." Having a private doctor on staff makes all the difference when things like this happen. My father's generation used a network of veterinarians for this purpose, but in today's age, organized crime has stepped up a notch at least.

"Give me fifteen minutes."

Manning hangs up before I can even admit that he might not have fifteen minutes, but I don't want to say that in front of him anyway. I pour a few fingers of whiskey into the glass Allie used tonight and thrust it into David's hand. He slurs a thank you and knocks back a large gulp before resuming his story with jagged breaths.

"Drink," I tell him, knowing it will help him relax. I set the bottle on the coffee table next to where he's slumped on the couch for easy refills and watch his pale face drip with sweat.

"You gotta get him. He can't do this to me and just walk." David's hand trembles as he brings the glass to his lips again. I'm well aware of my need to exterminate this pest, and with Allie out of harm's way now, I can do just that. I'd have been very content to keep her safely hidden away here or heavily guarded each time she left my home. Now, I have personal recourse to take the fight to him. No one harms my men and gets away with it.

"You need to stop talking and just drink the whiskey." I lift his hand back up and he tips the glass up at his lips. The more he drinks the more relaxed he'll be when Manning has to pull that slug out. This process repeats several more times while we wait, and during that time Lenny strolls in with blood all over his hands too. The two of us keep pressure on David's wound until Manning walks in.

I step away, leaving the mess to them and the cleaners I'll have to call in. Allie's ex just ruined my plans tonight. I am supposed to be heading out in a car to take out the scumbag who has a bead on Red. That has now become a low priority—to me at least. I dial Matty's number as I head toward my bedroom to check on Allie.

74

"Yeah, man, it's late. What do you want?" Matty sounds like he's been sleeping already, which is surprising. It's not that late.

"I'm handing Red over to you. The guy owes Dom big time, but he isn't paying up. That and the fact that Red pushed some sort of button he has means he's got to go. He's a loose cannon. Handle it within a week, before he makes his move." I walk faster, frustration coursing through my body. The only thing worse than having to hand over a hit is handing it over to one of my brothers.

"I thought you dealt with that already." Matty yawns and I hear a woman's voice in the background. I'm getting a better picture for what he's been doing all evening.

"Just do it."

I hang up and push the door to my bedroom open. Allie isn't in bed, and the bathroom door is open. I smell the faint scent of lavender and it draws me toward the bathroom. When I step into the doorway and lean on the jamb, I see Allie submerged in a bath, now probably cold. Her eyes are shut, her head lolled to the side. She's passed out.

I study the way the water distorts her curves, accentuating some, diminishing others. Those curves feel amazing against my body, and after this evening's romp, I'm hungry to know what other ways she can satisfy me.

"Sven?"

A tiny voice pulls me out of my mind. I turn to see Rico standing in the doorway of my room, and I pull the bathroom door shut and walk toward him. "What's up, bud?"

"I'm hungry. Do you have any snacks?" He rubs his eyes and I can tell he's tired. He's been in the game room for hours now. I crouch in front of him, uncertain what to do with a child. I've never been a nurturing type, but Allie isn't really in the position to come care for him and Marta is probably off to sleep already.

"Sure, kiddo. Let me call Gerard and he will get you whatever you want. You can sleep on the couch in the game room tonight, but I guess your mom doesn't want that to be your bedroom." I tousle his hair as I reach for my phone and shoot the butler a text message.

"Can I say goodnight to Mom?" He looks up at me and yawns again.

"She's having a bath. I'll tell her you said goodnight. You go on back to the game room and Gerard will bring you a snack. Did you meet Odin?" I stand and he nods.

"He's giant. I like him." Rico backs into the hallway. "I hope it's a good snack," he mumbles.

"I hope so too." I am ready to shut the door and go claim my bride from the bathtub but Rico is full of questions tonight.

"What about my dad? Why didn't you want me to go with him? Why doesn't my mom like him?"

Ten-thirty at night and this kid needs to open Pandora's box. I clench my jaw and glance at the open bathroom door. I don't know how much Rico knows about his father or what to say to him. Allie is passed out and useless. I don't want to deal with this tonight.

"Your dad is not a nice person. He hurt your mom pretty badly. She's worried he will hurt you too." I offer the most diplomatic answer possible. Rico looks thoughtful for a moment then nods.

"Does that mean you're a nice person?" His defiant attitude shines through. It could be a trait he picked up from his father via heredity, or he could have learned it from Allie. God knows she's a little stubborn. I like it. It reminds me of myself when I was young.

"Nice is relative kid. All you need to know is, you're safe here. You'll have everything you want and need to grow up healthy and happy, and your mom will be taken care of now." I cross my hands over my belt and pray his questions are over now.

"I'd say that's nice." He turns and takes a few steps down the hallway, then looks over his shoulder and says, "Thanks for letting me game in your room. I'm going to like it here." Then, he's gone.

I shake my head and shut the door, then head back into the bathroom. The night has been far more eventful than I'd have liked it to be for their first night here, but Rico was kept from the worst of it at least. Allie should never have seen David like that, and she will have questions for sure. I crouch next to the bathtub and watch her sleeping peacefully for a moment. She had far too much to drink.

"Hey," I say in a low tone, but she doesn't stir. I stick a finger into the water, not as cool as I thought it would be. She had to have started out with scalding hot temps in order for it to be this warm still. Marta probably found her wandering the hallway naked and led her here and sent her to the bath.

I glance up at the counter where a wash rag and bar of soap are sitting. She hasn't even bathed. She probably just sank into the water and passed out. I take the rag and dip it into the bath water, then rub the soap on it, sudsing it up. When it has a nice suds, I wash her carefully, starting with her breasts and armpits, working my way down her body. She stirs slowly, moaning and blinking her eyes open.

"Sven?" she mumbles.

"Shh, you fell asleep in the bath." I push the rag over her stomach, down over her shaven mound and between her legs. She groans, arching her back. Her tits push up out of the water, hard peaks forming. As I wash her, I remember the panties, stuffed inside her to keep her from dripping.

"Oh," she hums, prying her eyes open. "God... my neck."

"Yes, you passed out with your head at an awkward angle." I chuckle, then push a finger into her, searching for the lacy panties. I find them just as she grips my wrist. Hooking a finger around the material, I begin to pull it out, drawing soft gasps of pleasure from her lips. The fabric scratches across her skin little by little until it pulls free.

"Not again," she moans, and I can't help but wonder if she was dreaming of me. I use the wash rag to clean her, though I'd rather be slipping my fingers through her silky folds instead. And when she is clean, I pull the plug and reach for a towel. She stands up on wobbly legs, slipping on the tile as she climbs out of the bath. I wrap my arms and the towel around her to steady her and she lays her head on my chest. Tomorrow she may regret this, but tonight I am enjoying it.

I lead her to the bed and turn it down with one arm while I help her balance with the other. Her eyes are shut again, her face resting against my skin. I'm not used to giving this level of care to anyone. I've lived my entire life as a leader with maids and nannies as a child, and a full staff since I bought my first home at 25. Women who come into my life are here to serve me, not the other way around.

Allie is different.

I carefully scoop her up and lay her on the bed, making sure she has a pillow beneath her head so she doesn't wake up in more pain. Then I pull the covers over her body, but she kicks them off right away.

"Hot," she mumbles, before curling up into a ball. That explains how she was comfortable in the lukewarm bath. Rolling my eyes at her, I walk across the room and sit down to have a cigar and watch her sleep. It appears I'm going to need to up my game for this bastard. There is no way I'm letting him anywhere near her ever again. She's mine now, and I protect my property.

11

ALLIE

I blink my eyes open, unaware of what time it is. The room is lit, and I'm cold, still naked from my bath. My hand is pressed between my thighs, fingers dipping into my slit, which is caked in thick moisture. Was it a dream? Sven washing me in the bathtub? Or was that real. I touch myself lightly, feeling aroused by the thought of him finding me bathing and washing me.

My head still swims with alcohol, and I realize I can't have been sleeping that long. I probably passed out in the bath and the maid helped me into bed or something. I need to remember to thank her for that later on. For now, I enjoy the silky feeling of my swollen clit and the way my moisture makes my fingers slide across my skin. God, I'm so aroused.

"You enjoy that?"

Sven's voice is gruff, distinctly close to me too. I freeze, not realizing he has been watching me and then I push myself up to a sitting position. My nipples are hard, not from arousal, just from the cold air in the room. So he is the one who helped me to bed and he didn't even cover me up? Funny how when I realize it was him my gratitude flies out the window.

"Why are you watching me?" I hiss, scooting up on the bed until my back has pressed hard against the headboard. I scramble to cover myself. No sense giving him a free show. He takes what he wants anyway. Not that I would complain, but I don't want him getting the idea that I'm softening to his demands. I just need protection. I have no intention of falling for him.

"I smoke a cigar before I lay down every night." He sits forward on the chair and I see his erect dick is not in his pants where it belongs. How long was I touching myself while I was sleeping? And was he masturbating to my sleep-play? I can't pull my eyes away from his crotch; his fingers touch it lightly, holding it upright.

"I don't see a cigar." I glance at the ashtray on the corner of the dresser next to where he's seated. There is no smoke rising. In fact, there is no smoke hanging in the air either. He is either lying to me or—

"I finished that an hour ago."

Figures… He was watching me sleep-play. I cringe inside, wishing I could undo the past few hours and not get in that bath. After witnessing that bleeding man—and then the way Sven shouted at me —I'm having major second thoughts. Though, my vagina isn't saying that right now.

"So you watched me sleep for an hour?" I ask, defiant. I may have agreed to his controlling proposal, but I don't have to be his slave. Wives are to be respected, not used or abused. That's a lesson Paul never learned and shame on me for waiting so long to leave him.

"Two actually," he says, putting his hand around his dick and stroking gently. "And when you were sleep-talking, it was kinda sexy. So you did this to me. The part where you touched yourself was really fucking hot. Icing on the cake."

Shame washes over me, forcing me to retreat into myself when I realize we are both horny and I am naked. This is his room. I am supposedly his fiancé, and even though I don't know him, I want him.

"Do you always sit around watching a woman sleep and touch yourself thinking of her?" I squirm, feeling the ache in my vagina grow worse. I shift the thick maroon blanket so I can pull it up higher across my chest and a breeze wafts across my valley, sending a cooling sensation in every location my juices have spread. It's a mess down there. Why does my pussy betray me by wanting him when he isn't even civilized about this thing? Even if this was an arranged marriage by today's standards, I'd be given more respect.

"Only for you." He stands, letting his slacks fall to the ground along with his boxers. He's hard—really hard, and it makes my pussy clench. He walks to the bed and folds the covers back on his side, then climbs in. When he shuts off the light and turns his back on me, I am instantly furious. He wants me. I saw his hard cock. Why is he acting like he is just going to sleep? Why does he just lie down like he doesn't have precum smeared all over his shaft?

"Did you wash me?" I ask, angry that he is just going to sleep. Doesn't he know I am horny? He has to know. He was watching me touch myself.

"Couldn't help myself. Besides, I didn't want that delicious pussy getting an infection. You forgot to take the panties out."

I wince and clench my jaw. He doesn't care about me. Why did he say that? He just wants a toy, or a trophy, though I can't see how I'd be a trophy to a man this wealthy. I'm nothing to him, just a human blow-up doll he can order around. That doesn't stop my pussy from needing fucked though.

"You've got to be kidding me." I cross my arms over my chest in a huff and growl out my frustration.

"What?" he asks, turning to look over his shoulder at me. In the darkness I can just make out a smirk on his face. He's toying with me, pushing my buttons.

"You're just going to sleep?"

Why am I being so forward with him? Is it the alcohol I'm clearly still under the effects of? Or has this man gotten under my skin so badly that I can't stand to be at peace around him?

"I was planning to. That's what you do in a room with the lights off after midnight." He turns back and adjusts his pillow and I scream growl.

I pull my pillow out from behind my back and smack him with it hard. Big mistake. He comes off the bed in a flash, turning and yanking me down toward the foot of the bed by my ankles. "What the hell are you doing? Who do you think you are?" Sven is strong, stronger than Paul. I tremble there at the edge of the bed, waiting to see if he'll fuck me or smack me.

"Your toy apparently," I spit out, trying to back away, but he grips both of my hips and pins me down. He's strong enough to manhandle me any way he wants, and it's a rush feeling his fingers dig into my sides. Definitely the alcohol.

"If you were just a toy, I'd have never let you sleep. You'd have been bruised from pussy to knee with how hard I fucked you." His breath is hot against my skin as he growls his words into my ears.

"Then fucking do it," I tell him, shuddering to think of that wild of a sexual experience. I believe he's capable of it—of making me cum so hard every blood vessel in my lower half bursts with the pressure of orgasmic contractions. I kinda want to feel that.

"You're not ready, Princess."

"I'm not a Princess." I try to get one last point against him, but my body is lying to me. Every part of me is on fire for this man. He's not even inside me and I'm shaking with the need for him. How can someone I barely know have such control over me?

"Now go to sleep," he growls, pulling my body tight against his and wrapping his arms around me as he crawls back into bed. I feel him from my shoulders to the backs of my thighs, and his hard dick presses against me. Teasing me.

"I'm not tired," I tell him defiantly, crossing my arms over my chest.

"I didn't say you were. I said, sleep."

He's got me. I can't think when I'm under his arms. I'm his toy, and if I'm not careful, I'll just be a body to him. I need to make sure I'm more than that.

"I'm not going to sleep," I tell him, my arms unclenching from across my chest. My hands unfurl over his broad shoulders and I run my fingernails down his chest and over his abs, watching the muscles of his stomach jump and quiver under my touch. My hands are antsy, and I'm not sure how long I'll be able to resist touching him.

"You don't want to sleep?" he asks, his body tensing as I gently scratch up and down his torso. I can feel his eyes watching my hands, but I don't look up to meet them. I just keep my eyes focused on my hands, watching as my nails and fingers play over his skin.

"No," I whisper, closing my eyes and letting my hands move over his body. "I want to make you come."

The invitation is sent and I'm waiting on the RSVP when his dick slides between my legs and into my mess. "You don't know what you want. You're drunk."

"Fuck me," I growl, biting his arm. I grind against his dick, letting his thick girth slip through my slit. "Now."

Sven rocks his hips upward, forcing his dick between my legs hard. His pelvis slams into mine, and I know what he means by "bruised from pussy to knees." I want it so bad. I lift a leg and drape it over his body and reach between my legs to guide him into me. At this angle, he feels thick, but it's not deep enough to give me the sensation I had earlier—him slamming into my womb. I want that.

"Shit... You are huge," I moan, clawing at his sides. Each time he thrusts in I gasp again. I kegel, tightening my pussy around him, whimpering for more.

"You like it rough?" Sven asks, rolling on top of me. He grabs both of my wrists and pins them over my head, then leans down to bite my nipple, hard. I yelp and wrap my legs around his waist as he fucks me. The entire bed shakes.

"Yes, fuck me hard," I groan, feeling him fill me and retreat over and over.

"You're a bad girl, Allie. You need a real fucking to work out some of that attitude." His cock feels like it's tearing me, and my moans of pleasure get louder.

"Yes, fuck me like a bad girl," I whimper. "I'm a bad girl for you, Sven. Fuck me like a bad girl."

"You like it... when I fuck you like a bad girl?" Sven asks, his breath hitching. He's close. The way his hands grip me tightly hurts almost, but I don't resist or complain. I want more.

"I love it," I moan, feeling my entire body shudder.

"But you're a good girl, aren't you? You'll be a good girl for me," Sven says, thrusting into me deep. His skin slaps against mine; it sounds like he's smacking me.

"Oh, God, I'm coming, I'm coming, I'm coming..." I mewl, my pussy clenching around him and squeezing his dick. I spasm, my back arching off the bed. I'm a trembling mess as I come. "Oh, fuck me, fuck me..."

"I'm fucking you," Sven growls, still thrusting until I'm so limp my entire body shakes the way my tits bounce with his thrusts. He pulls out, hastily grabbing my hips and flipping me over. "Fuck, I am going to enjoy this."

His cock slides through my juices, up and down my crack, and he taps it on my ass cheek. I know what's coming. I'm not ready. I whimper in panic as the head of his dick presses against my hot entrance. "Sven... I..." I moan, but he's there, stretching me. The tight ring of muscles gives way to his pressure, forcing a scream from my mouth. I bury my face on the pillow as he sinks into me, fingers clawing at my sides.

"Oh, fuck yeah..." His thrusting begins again, his giant cock nearly tearing me from ass to pussy. I thought he stretched my pussy out but this is so intense I'm clawing at the bedsheets praying to god I don't pass out. He's massive and he's going to tear me.

"Sven..." I mutter, then bite down on the pillow. He's not stopping, but strangely, it doesn't hurt as bad anymore. In fact, it's starting to feel good. Amazing even. I touch myself, swirling my fingers around my clit, stimulating the sensation there.

I moan and pant, pulling my face away from the pillow. He reaches around my body and pushes my hand out of the way, finding my clit. "Your ass is mine now. Just like your pussy. No one else will ever touch it again." His demanding words tingle my spine.

"Say it again," I pant, realizing he is going to make me come again.

"That you're mine? That my cock is the only cock that will ever go in you again? Because it's true." Sven reaches for my wrist and grabs it, guiding my hand to my clit. With his body slamming into mine, it's hard to balance, but I touch myself, bringing myself to the edge as he fucks me.

I don't even expect what he does next. My head jerks back as he grabs a handful of my hair and pulls it. "Come now," he growls. "You're mine. No one else's. Say it!" With my head arched back like this it's difficult to even breathe. The world around me dims and I suck in a hard breath.

"I'm yours!" I cry out. "My pussy, my ass... they're yours!" My orgasm tears through me as he fucks me through it. My body is so limp I can barely stay conscious. I float somewhere between the world of deep sleep and another orgasm when I feel his hand smack down on my ass.

"You have the most beautiful ass on the planet," he growls. "And it's all mine."

He reaches around my body, rubbing my clit as he keeps fucking me hard. I'm riding the edge of another orgasm. "Oh fuck, it's so good..." I call out as his hands grab my hips, lifting me up and slamming me backward on his dick. He pulls me up, his lips finding my neck. He sucks on it, hard, making me moan. I feel him bite down, and I cry out in pain.

"That's right," he growls, his teeth still sunk in me. "You're mine." His hands move up my body and grab my tits, pulling me down on him harder. I cry out in pleasure, feeling his cock sink deep inside of me. He slams into me three more times before moaning out and filling me with his seed.

I can feel him leaking out of me, and it's so good. I can feel my body milk his cum out, squeezing him. He pulls out, and his cum dribbles down my ass and thighs. It's hot and sticky and I collapse onto the bed hard. I can't breathe; sex was that amazing.

"You're a bad girl," Sven says, rolling off of me. I pant and roll over, staring at the ceiling.

This man has my head swimming. One second I am scared of him; the next I want him in my body like a volcano exploding. I can't catch my breath. What he just did to me hurt like hell and felt amazing all at once. The cummy mess I'm lying in feels disgusting, but I could fall asleep right now and sleep like a baby all night.

"Are you really going to make me marry you?" I ask, taking a deep breath and heaving it out. Sven wraps an arm around me and pulls me against his chest, and I turn away from him so he can spoon me. The action makes more of his cum ooze out of me. I'm going to need a shower in the morning.

"Yes, I am. You agreed to it."

I lie here wondering for a moment if he actually has feelings for me or what he's even thinking. Why does he just pick a woman off the street and say "That's the one I'm going to marry?" Has he never heard of romance, dating, love?

"And if I want to divorce you later on?" I reach for the covers, my sweat-glazed body beginning to take a chill. He covers me up, then tightly wraps his arm over my torso again. I actually enjoy the feeling of his warmth against my back as he holds me tightly. His answer is slow in coming, but he does answer.

His voice is low and gruff as he says, "You won't ever have the desire to do that, but if you do, you will be free to leave." He sounds almost dejected, and I feel sorry for him.

I contemplate what he means by that answer. Considering we don't know each other at all, I'd say there is a very high likelihood that I will want to divorce him in the near future. Just as soon as Paul is gone. Hell, I'm not even married to him yet and I want to divorce him. But I give him the benefit of the doubt and stop my prying questions. At least as far as the forced marriage is concerned.

"The man who was bleeding… Did he die? Who was he?"

I feel Sven tense as I ask the question, and he mumbles, "I think you should just focus on sleeping."

"Sven?"

"Mmm," he mutters, before he lets a yawn escape. His hot breath breezes across my cheek and I hesitate asking the next question, but it's one burning in my heart. I have to know.

"Are you going to hurt me like Paul did? Are you dangerous?" Now it's my turn to tense. He pulls away and the bed is instantly an icebox. It shakes, and I feel him leave the mattress entirely. I stifle the whine that wants to escape because I don't want to upset him more.

"I'm only dangerous to people who defy me or rebel. Now go to sleep." He walks into the bathroom and shuts the door, and I see the light stream from beneath the thick wood.

Before I can put logical thought to the answer he gave me, my eyes shut, heavy with sleep. My breathing regulates; I hug the comforter to my chest and relax my shoulders. Sleep comes swiftly.

At least the sex is amazing...

1 2

SVEN

Things are a mess. Shipments aren't being received properly; orders aren't being tracked. And I'm not talking about the raw fish sales we process through this facility. Dominic is going to be furious when he finds out and he's going to blame me. I've been spending so much time trying to keep Allie out of harm's way my duties are slipping.

I slam my fist on the desk in the front office and the pens in the cup dance. Jen shakes, startled by my outburst and stares up at me with saucer eyes, scared. After dealing with the mess Allie's ex made for me with David and Lenny, I am in no mood to read how far behind we are with things. Trouble has been brewing a while anyway, but now under my watch I'm going to be responsible to fix it and I just don't have time. Not until I make that bastard pay for shooting my guy.

"Sir, I only did what Nick told me. The numbers are straight; we just didn't—"

"Enough!" I snap, cutting her off. I'm livid now, the kind of anger that makes me want to be violent. Nothing has gone my way for days and I feel like a caged lion. "No excuses. You get Fischer on the phone and tell him to pay the invoice now or he will get a visit from Rome. And don't take no for an answer."

"But sir, Rome is—"

Just my glare silences her this time. My younger brother ties up loose ends and that's what he'll do if I give the order. "Where is Nick?"

After he tried to manipulate me into going behind Dom's back the other day, the damn bastard ignored what I told him and did what he wanted anyway. The numbers don't lie. I don't care how many millions we stand to profit if there isn't loyalty in the family then there is nothing. Money doesn't go into your grave with you.

"Sir, I don't know. He and Leo were talking earlier about taking lunch at Amelio's." Jen trembles as she speaks, a sure sign my screaming has gotten through to her. I scowl and head off toward the production floor with hands clenched into fists. The door slams into something as I push it open, sending gun parts flying across the room. Several of my guys look up in surprise, a few of them chuckling.

"Nick!" I shout, scanning the floor. I see the tow motor hauling a skid full of boxes toward the docs where a semi waits to be filled. Nick isn't there, and I don't see him around the fishing crates either. "Anyone seen Nick?" I call out only to receive a grumble of mixed answers.

"Back office, boss," one of the guys calls above the beeping of the tow motor, and I start that direction when I hear gunshots ring out. Everyone freezes and a few guys drop to the ground, but every one of us pulls our weapon and readies it for action.

"What the hell?"

"Who's shooting?"

"What was that?"

The chorus of shouts meets my ear, but I'm not at all surprised to hear it. I crouch behind a large barrel of fish oil and pull my gun, chambering a round. Dominic warned me about the attempt on his life, that someone was gunning for him and I believed him. I know this has to be connected. I hear shots coming from the hallway that leads to the back office, so I point at a few of my guys and gesture for them to follow me. Lenny nods and Rex falls in line with us.

"Stay low. We don't know what's happening yet." The instant the words leave my mouth, the hallway door bursts open and I see Nick barge in with guns blazing. He fires off several rounds in my direction.

"What the hell, boss?" Rex shouts before standing to take a few shots at Nick. "Why's he shooting at us?"

We all hunker down behind large pallets of fish vats. Any bullet fired at them will be stopped by the gelatinous fish and ice in the vats. Gunfire echoes overhead, bullets ricocheting off the walls. The tow motor driver stops the machine and slides off, pulling his weapon too. I expect him to take aim at Nick and blast a few rounds, but he points at us instead. His aim is true, striking Lenny in the shoulder.

"Fuck!" Lenny drops his weapon, now sprawling on the ground, and I stand and fire off four rounds in rapid succession, advancing on the driver until he drops to the ground, covered in blood. Nick takes the opportunity to fire off a few more shots, but his bullets hit the metal shelving I dodge between.

Rage clouds my vision. All I see is red. I turn the corner and lean out past the shelving, firing off several more rounds. I hit a few more men, though I'm not sure who is shooting who now. There are so many guns discharging, it's hard to tell in the cacophony who is on whose side. I pause, pulling back behind the shelf and notice Nick vanish out the door. Rex chases after him, but I'm hemmed in. I peek around the corner again and hear the whir of a bullet as it flies past my head. There are still several shooters, but there are also several men laid out on the ground writhing in pain.

"This is going to end in a lot of blood, Gusev." I hear a familiar voice but I can't place it. It's not any of the men I am closest to, which means it probably isn't a close family member.

"You and anyone on your side is going to die!" I whip around the corner, firing repeatedly as I advance out onto the floor. Men cower, dropping behind shelves and boxes. Every place I see movement I point and shoot, not even caring if I kill loyals at this point. Anyone who is not on my side is an enemy, and every last ounce of anger inside my chest is being unleashed.

"Sven!" I hear a shout and turn over my shoulder to see Matty with a gun in his hand. I also get a fast glimpse of a gun pointed at me and I drop to my knee, narrowly missing another bullet. Matty pulls the trigger of his gun, dropping the bastard who tried to shoot me and I pop back to my feet. When I round the next corner with hasty steps, I find myself staring down the barrel of a gun held by a woman I don't recognize. She's young, probably in her mid-twenties, with long dark hair that falls down her back in waves. Her eyes are cold and calculating, and I can tell she's not here to play games.

I raise my own gun, feeling the weight of it in my hand as I try to gauge the situation. This woman is no ordinary thug -- she's got something about her that sets her apart from the others. I can tell she's been trained, and trained well.

"Who the hell are you?" I demand, keeping my gun trained on her chest.

She doesn't answer, just stares me down with those icy eyes. I can feel the tension in the air, thick and heavy and dangerous. This woman is a wildcard, and I don't know what she's capable of.

But I'm not one to back down from a fight. I take a step forward, narrowing the distance between us, and she doesn't flinch. She's not scared of me, that's for damn sure. But I can see the wheels turning in her head, the calculations she's making about how to take me down.

I don't give her the chance. I fire off a shot, aiming for her shoulder, but she's quick. She ducks out of the way, her own gun pointed at my head now. I can feel the rush of adrenaline coursing through my veins, my heart pounding in my chest. I duck behind a shelf and check my gun, only two rounds left. If I miss, I'm dead, unless Matty gets to her first.

"Matty!" I shout, and hear the rapid recall of his weapon discharging, and I know he's fighting for his life. I have to get to him, and fast. But this woman is standing in my way, and she's not going to let me pass without a fight.

I peek out from behind the shelf and see her moving towards me, her gun still pointed at my head. I know what I have to do. With a deep breath, I lunge out from behind the shelf and tackle her to the ground. We roll around on the concrete floor, fighting for control of the gun. I can feel her strength, and I know I'm in for a tough fight.

But I'm not going to let her win. With a sudden burst of energy, I push her off me and stand up. "Who are you?" I demand, my voice shaking with adrenaline.

She spits in my face, and her spittle is followed by blood, a lot of it. A bullet hits her in the back of the head, splattering her brain matter onto my face and chest, and I lower my weapon, thinking it's over. A flash of movement in the corner of the room catches my eye, and I raise my weapon and fire off my last two rounds quickly, my gun now empty. I drop to my knee as Matty handles the final rebel and I breathe a sigh of relief.

I'm still kneeling there catching my breath when Matty runs up to me. "Sven, you okay?" he asks, offering a hand.

"I'm fine," I snap, ignoring his hand and standing. I push past him and walk toward the dock where I saw Nick run out earlier. That bastard is behind all of this. I know it. And he's going to pay. I check my gun again, releasing the slide, furious I have no rounds left. I'll just have to strangle him with my bare hands.

"Sven, dude, you shot at your own men without thinking." Matty follows me like a yappy ankle biter, and I ignore him, moving more swiftly as I pass dead bodies dropped like flies. "Fucking stop, Sven," he screams, and I turn around with my gun pointed right at his head. He holds his hands up defensively and shakes his head. "Woah!"

"Shut the hell up. You got that?" Every cell in my body is on fire with hatred for Nick. Dominic trusted me to run this shipping yard and I put too much trust in a weasel who was out for blood. Now he's going to pay. I just have to find him.

"Sven, calm down. You know if Dom saw you he'd—"

"Fuck Dominic. This is my yard and I'm handling things." I turn and lower my gun. I hear a single shot outside and wonder what that's about. When I push the door open, Matty following me out, I see Rom and Leo already moving toward the sound of the gunshot. It's coming from the alley around the corner. I take a few quick steps to catch up with them.

"Fuck, Sven, what happened?" Rome is checking his gun, most likely out of ammunition too.

"Nick came in shooting. Half our guys in there are dead, some friendly, some not. I have no fucking clue what happened." I use the back of my sleeve to wipe that woman's blood off my face and feel the scratching of some sort of bone across my skin. Rivulets of sweat stream down the sides of my face and I taste a hint of coppery flavor as her blood is rinsed by my perspiration.

"Who was that woman?" Matty asks, now falling into step with the rest of us.

"I have no clue," I snap, jamming my gun into my waistband.

"That brunette? Nick's woman. She's been hanging around here barking orders. Word has it she works with the Albanians." Rome points at a car up ahead, and I see Dominic standing there with a woman clinging to him. He's bleeding. "What happened there?"

"Dom?" Matty calls, rushing up to him. The rest of us fall into place, surrounding Dominic and his girlfriend. Nick is dead on the ground, the angle of the gun and the way his mouth gapes open tells me Dom forced him to kill himself.

"Guys," Dom says, his voice husky. He's not mortally wounded, but he's in pain. I can see it in his expression. I say nothing. I know this is largely my fault. If I had been paying better attention to things down here instead of chasing tail, I'd have seen Nick's plan way sooner. As it was, no one else even knew there was a mole, only Dominic and me.

"Rome, get them home. Leo, cops are going to be on this scene in a matter of minutes. There is no time for cleaners. Just get Detective Sikes on it. And Matty, get me something to wipe my face." With Dominic injured, I have to step up, but all I want to do is step away. All of this has made my anger toward Allie's ex even hotter.

Matty rushes away and returns with a damp cloth, and I wipe my face clean. He looks annoyed and a little intimidated, maybe because I held a gun to his head. I don't know. "What?" I snap, throwing the rag at him. I need to get out of here before the police show up because I have a record. If they know I was involved, I'll end up back in the clink.

"Look, I lost that guy. The one you said to take out. He's in the wind." Matty runs a hand through his sweat-soaked hair and kicks a rock. "I'm sorry, man. I totally dropped the ball."

"And Red? Holy fuck, Matt. What the hell? I ask you to do one simple job and you screw it up!" I shove him hard and he backs away. I'm letting my anger get the better of me again. I need to walk away before I hurt my brother, so I do.

Dominic is going to ream me for sure now. All of this is coming down on my head. There is no way out of it. I storm off, heading for my car. Sirens in the distance warn me my time here is up. I pass several police cars on my way out, lights flashing and sirens blaring. The entire shipping yard is lit up like Christmas.

When I get home Allie is there. I no more than get in the door when she starts grilling me. Her feet slap on the tile as she follows me through the front foyer into my den and I shed my coat.

"You're covered in blood. What the hell is going on? Are you hurt?" Her concern doesn't sound genuine, but then I am coercing her into marrying me, so I don't expect her to be nurturing just yet.

"It's someone else's," I growl, reaching for my bottle of aged Scotch.

"That's not!" she says pointing at my arm. I look down at my left bicep and notice blood there. I don't even feel pain, but I've been hit. With a swift yank, I tear the sleeve right off the ruined shirt and use it to wipe away the blood so I can see the wound better.

"It's just a scratch from some metal on a shelf or something." I lie to her because she didn't need to know what happened.

"And the blood on your face?" she snarls, arms crossed over her chest accusingly as she watches me finish pouring my drink.

"Fish blood." I hold the cup up to her, offering her a drink and she glares at me.

"What do you do for a living, Sven? Because I can't be with another violent man." Her nasty tone pushes buttons I didn't know I have. I down the entire glass of whiskey and set the glass down so hard it shatters.

"I told you last night, I'm not like him. I'm not going to hurt you." As if the questioning last night wasn't bad enough, she's just rubbing salt in a wound. She has no idea what I've just been through so I try to stay calm, but I'm so worked up, I could literally throw her out and not think twice.

"You know I left him because he was violent. Now you have bleeding men in your house. You come home soaked in someone else's blood. You're injured and—"

I snap, lurching toward her and grabbing her by the neck. Before I realize what I'm doing ,she's pinned against the bookshelf and I'm staring her down. "I said, I'm not like him." I loosen my grip, letting her go, but I don't back off. "Now, you can either calm the fuck down and let me relax, or you can pack your shit and go back on the street where I found you and defend yourself against that asshole."

Her eyes search me and I can see her chest pounding, a pulsing vein in her neck throbbing as she gathers her thoughts. I will not stoop to his level. It's the one thing I will never do. I won't harm her or control her, but she will respect me.

13

ALLIE

"I'm sorry." Sven has a temper—mental note of that for future reference. I know what it's like to push those buttons. I have seen Paul erupt on a moment's notice. At least it took Sven a bit of nudging. I need to know what he's into though. My anxiety is too high, my fear too fresh. Whatever he does for a living is dangerous; the blood is too much evidence to the fact. For all I know he's just a cop or a detective of some sort, and I'm just being overly dramatic, but it's not like I haven't been in a relationship with a violent man before. I can't repeat that. There is no point in staying with him if he's just like Paul.

But like Paul, Sven must have some sort of means of stress relief, some way I can help him relax and loosen up so he will talk to me. I've gone about this the wrong way. He clearly won't respond to me being pushy or demanding.

"How can I help you relax? It was insensitive of me to think I could demand answers of you like that. I should have been more sensitive." I move toward him, gently touching the wound on his arm. "Should I have a look? This needs cleaned or it will get infected."

"It's fine," he grumbles, ignoring the stream of blood trickling down his bicep. He walks away, moving toward the liquor cabinet and pouring himself a drink.

"Then, maybe you want me to rub your shoulders? Maybe I can refill your drinks." I follow him, offering to take the bottle, but he clutches it tightly in his fist and carries it to the coffee table. I follow him, amazed by how the blood that had been smeared all over this sofa yesterday is completely gone. I'd have never known a bleeding man sat here.

"A good fuck helps me relax," he says smugly, propping his feet on the table. He downs the whiskey in the glass and sets the glass on the table, but keeps the bottle in hand. His eyes train on me as I follow him, perching on the leather armchair at the end of the coffee table. Sex wasn't what I was offering, but I probably have no choice.

"Yeah?" I ask him nervously. It's amazing sex, don't get me wrong; I just want answers, not orgasms right now. "You're not hungry? Maybe a hot shower. I could help you take care of the wound."

"You want me to relax or see a doctor?" He tips the bottle up to his lips and takes a long swig. Bubbles rise through the honey-colored liquid until he lowers it.

"Of course I want you to relax."

"Then take off your clothes and let me watch you." Sven leans forward, setting the whiskey down on the table and screwing the cap back on, which was clutched in his palm. I swallow hard, knowing I have to put on some sort of performance, though his demanding tone is quite arousing. I've always loved a very assertive man, which is probably how I ended up with an abuser.

"Take off your clothes," he demands again, his voice low and husky. "I want to watch you."

I swallow hard and peel off my shoes. I set them on the armchair, then unbutton my jeans and wiggle out of them. I fold those, and set them next to my shoes. I'm wearing a white t-shirt which I pull over my head. When his fingers point at my bra and panties and he flicks it to the side, indicating he wants them removed too, I obey. My body is starting to respond to this level of assertiveness in a way I don't expect.

I stand there for a moment, nervously. I'm not shy about my body, but I'm not in front of a man who wants to be seduced. I'm in front of a man who wants to control me, and I'm going to have to play along.

"Come here," he growls. I walk closer, but stop a few feet away. He looks at my chest, to my hips, at my legs, and then his eyes travel back up to my face. He looks me in the eye, and then his gaze drops to the floor. "Turn around, and show me your ass."

He's not smiling or joking. I turn around, and I can feel his eyes on me.

"Spread your feet apart," he says.

I do, and I feel his hands on my hips. I feel his fingers dig into the skin there. And then I feel him push me forward. I step out of his hands, and I move forward a few more inches.

"Bend," he says. I bend forward, so my hands are on the floor. His hands are on my hips again, and they move down over the curve of my ass and to my knees. I can feel the heat of his breath as it hits the back of my thighs. I'm still bent over when I feel his fingers slide up my inner thigh. I tremble slightly, then freeze as his hand slides between my legs.

"What a pretty little, tight pussy," he says. His voice is low and rough. His hand slips into my slit, and his fingers begin to move. They slide up and down, parting my lips and moving over my clit. I'm starting to get wet. I moan softly.

"Fuck, I bet you taste amazing," Sven growls, pushing a single finger into my pussy. I shudder, wanting more. How does he do this to me every time? And then I feel his hands, gripping my ass cheeks. He pushes them apart, and I feel the heat of his breath on my pussy. I'm nervous, but I'm turned on too.

"Oh, yes," he whispers, and his tongue slides up my slit. He starts to lap at me, and I can hear him enjoying my juices. His tongue is moving faster, and he's making me tremble. Then he shifts, and I feel his fingers on my asshole. His tongue is teasing my clit, and his fingers are teasing the tight ring of muscles. I lean back, pressing into them. I want more.

"Do you like that?" he growls. Sven smears my moisture around, slicking all of my skin. It's torture, the way he teases me and plays with my clit at the same time.

"Mmmhmm," I moan. I back into him harder, wanting to be penetrated and he reads my mind.

"I bet you'd like to get fucked, wouldn't you?"

He slips a finger into my pussy, and then a second finger. I'm moaning and gasping, arching my back and pressing into his fingers.

"You'd like to get fucked, wouldn't you?" he asks again.

"Yess," I moan.

"Good girl," he says softly. His hands leave my body, and I hear him unzip his pants. A moment later, and I feel him behind me. His cock is pressing against my slit and then sliding up into me. He's fucking me slowly.

"Mmm, yes," he growls. He puts his hands on my hips, holding me in place as he thrusts. He's going deep, so deep it takes my breath away. He's taking his time, and I'm moaning and gasping.

"You like being fucked, don't you?" he whispers.

"Yes," I moan.

"You like me fucking you, don't you?"

LYDIA HALL

"Mmm, yes," I mumble.

"Then tell me what you want."

"I want you to cum inside me," I gasp. His rigid dick grinds into my cervix massaging it. It feels like he wants to make his deposit directly into my womb, and fuck if it isn't an amazing feeling. I grip my knees and try to keep my balance.

"What?"

"I want you to cum inside me," I moan again.

"Beg me," he growls.

"Please cum inside me," I moan, my voice high and tight.

"Please fuck me," he says, his voice harsh.

"Fuck me," I moan, my voice high.

"I'm going to fuck you so hard," he whispers.

"And then you'll tell me who you really are..." I moan, knowing this is pushing his buttons as much as it is mine, but I don't get what I expect. Sven falls silent, his fingers finding my clit and pinching and twisting it as he slams into me.

He hits my body so hard, I begin to convulse around him, strong, powerful contractions that grip his cock so hard he has a hard time pushing into me. He begins to fuck me harder, like he's fighting for his breath. He's pounding me now, and I'm moaning and gasping and clenching around him. He's fighting to hold back, and I'm fighting to hold back, and we're both losing.

"Please," I moan.

"Please what?" he growls.

"Please, cum in me," I beg.

"You'd like that, wouldn't you?" he growls. "You need to be punished, Allie. Because you need to learn to mind your own business."

He's fucking me hard and fast, his cock pounding into me, and there's nothing I can do about it. I'm gasping and moaning and trying to keep from screaming. I can't help but come again, because he's holding back. The only thing I can do is hold onto him, and I do. I hold on to him and I moan and I breathe.

When he finally floods me, and the heat of his explosion dribbles down my inner thigh, I'm spent. I can't even begin to think about pressing him for more information. I collapse to my knees on the wood floor, panting, and I hear him zip his pants back up.

"Yeah, that was relaxing," he says, and I hear his footsteps move away from me and the slosh of whiskey in the bottle. Then he's gone.

I remain there on my knees a while; I'm not sure how long. His cum puddles on the floor beneath my legs. I let it. I'm not the maid, and I'm not cleaning his mess up. Especially when he disarms me like that. Who does he think he is using sex a means to bring me to my knees—literally? I know nothing about him, not where he works or what he does, not even his last name. These are things a fiancé should know about the man she'll marry.

Pushing myself off the floor, I collect my clothing and dress. The mess between my legs is sticky and makes me feel gross. I'll shower tonight, but not until I talk to Sven. He needs to understand that if I am going to stick to this agreement, I need to know what he really does for a living. The arrangement is crazy enough to begin with, but throw in a bit of violence and bloodshed and I'm a lunatic for agreeing to it. I'd be better off with Paul. At least he hid nothing. He was himself through and through.

With my clothing in place, I make my way toward the bedroom. I can hear the faint hint of gunshots reverberating down the stairs and know Rico is playing one of his first-person-shooter games. While violent, at least I know he's safe; they're not real guns and I can turn them off any time I choose with a push of a button. Sven, however, I have no control over, and he plays with fire.

The bedroom door is cracked, so I push it open and walk in. Sven is stretched across the bed, leaning on the headboard staring at the television mounted on the wall above the dresser. He glances at me but says nothing, and I shut the door quietly behind myself. I move toward the bed and he looks up at me again. I can see the glaze of alcohol over his eyes, but the blood flow on his arm has stopped.

"Is Rico liking the game room?" he asks me. Surprisingly, his words are not slurred at all. He lounges like a king. He hasn't even changed out of his blood-soiled clothing. At least he removed his shoes.

I perch on the edge of the mattress, feeling the moisture between my legs. It's gross, but I keep a straight face, knowing I'll wash it off soon. "He really enjoys it. I spent a little time with him earlier. He also really likes Odin; he's always wanted a dog." My hand falls to my knee where I pick at a loose thread on the side of my jeans.

"Good," he grunts, turning his attention back to the television.

"Sven..." I take a deep breath and bolster my confidence. "I'm not going to pry any more about what you do for a living. Just promise me you aren't in some gang or something."

"I'm not in a gang," he says curtly. "I'm watching TV. Can't this wait?"

"I want to go back to work." I know he's already told me it wasn't going to happen, but I never expected to have to change who I am just because I'm getting married. "I miss my friends. I need to get out of the house and do things."

"It's too dangerous."

"But—"

"The answer is no." He doesn't even look at me, doesn't care that I have desires.

I stand and move toward the bathroom, half-expecting him to call me back but he doesn't. I'm angry, but after that display I know better than to question him. So I step into the bathroom and start to undress. The door is open a crack, though it was unintentional, so when his phone rings curiosity gets the better of me. I lean against the wall, standing there naked, and listen to what he says.

"Red… What do you mean he was shot…? Dead…? Fuck's sake, Dom." That last comment was anger, plain and simple. "Motherfuckers are going to pay…"

And at that word, I realize I'm in over my head. Who is Red? And why was he shot? Sven must be involved with very dangerous people and I want nothing to do with it. Rico and I can't stay here. Even if it means risking things with Paul. I want out.

14

SVEN

The room is tense, emotions raw. All four of my brothers stand near my father, who is seated with his can in his hand. He can barely walk now, and Dominic has for all intents and purposes become the leader. Still, Dad showed his face today to honor Red, slaughtered in the hunt for the mole who is now also dead, only a few hours too late.

"You did well, Dominic," Dad says, his voice still heavy with his Russian accent. Dad immigrated here with his parents, who only spoke Russian, but all of us boys were born here. First generation Americans and one of the most powerful families in the city. We all look to Dominic as our leader, and he nods at Dad with respect.

"It came at a cost. We lost so many good men today." Dominic's shoulders are squared, but I can tell by the tone of his voice that his heart is heavy. Red was dear to all of us, me especially. We were pretty close in age, and he was my go-to guy for so many things, including heart to heart talks. I'm going to miss that bastard more than I even know.

"It shouldn't have happened, that is for sure," Dad slurs. "How did we let this go so long?" His eyes turn upward at Leo, the second oldest.

Leo's head hangs in shame, his shoulders dropping like a wilting plant. Nick was his best friend and he never saw it for a single second.

"He had us all fooled," Dominic tells Leo, gripping his shoulder.

"But he was my best friend." I watch Leo's fists tighten and loosen as he fights himself. "I should have seen it."

"There is an old saying," my father chimes in, "that says 'Keep your friends close and your enemies closer.' It reminds us that we should know all things at all times from all people. If they are not your friend, they are your enemy. Your mistake was thinking Nick was a friend and suspecting others. This family must scrutinize everyone at all times because power like we have does not come cheap—" Dad's words are cut off as he begins coughing. His coughs shake his whole body, and Rome, the youngest, hands Dad a handkerchief.

We wait for him to settle. It's tough watching my father suffer, but it is the process of life. He reminds us this every time we show a trace of emotion about his impending death. Each of us stands with great heaviness, but other than Leo none of us show it in our body language. We are men, bred to be leaders and demand respect.

"Dad is right. We all have a great deal of responsibility to trust no one. We must protect our family name and the power that comes along with it. Nick was a parasite amongst us, but he's gone. Now we rebuild. No one is to be trusted, because we don't know who left may have been loyal to him. Everyone must be vetted again, and we must bind together." Dominic put his fist into his palm and ground them together.

One of my aunts, sister to my late mother, pushes her way into the circle and sobs on my father's shoulder for a moment. Red meant nothing to her, but like a moth to the flame, she flits about the money and power in this room every chance she gets. Dad dismisses her, and Leo guides her away, and we are left with another coughing fit. The handkerchief in Dad's hand is peppered with blood, a sign that his condition is worse than we all know, but he will never let on. He folds the handkerchief and tucks it into his breast pocket.

"This is all nonsense," he says, waving his hand in the air. His fingers are curled slightly, thin skin revealing every vein beneath its translucent surface. "When I die you all know what I want." He shakes his finger at each of us, just as Leo returns to take his place. "You turn me to ash and pour me off the Brooklyn Bridge. Set my soul to rest where I feel most at home—the sea."

I've heard the speech a hundred times, at every funeral we've endured since the time my mother was laid to rest when I was just a teen.

"And don't have a ridiculous ceremony. Move on with life. Death is final; no need to commemorate it with meals and gatherings." He uses his cane to stand, forcing his weak body upward. Leo is there for support but Dad waves him off. He feebly wobbles his way toward the door and Leo, Rome, and Matty follow him out the door.

Dominic and I stand like sentry's next to Red's casket for another hour, allowing all the mourners to pay their final respects before his body is taken to the cemetery. Dad refused to have a graveside service, so only Dominic will attend the body. When the last of our relatives passes by, I ask Dominic the question I've been waiting all day to get an answer for.

"So this new guy, Jimmy... You honestly think we can trust him?" I don't look at my brother as I speak. I'm irritated by his choice of replacing Red with an outsider. Jimmy Slater is not blood. He's not even Russian. Hell, I don't even know if he's not just some plant from one of our enemies—or worse, a cop.

"You heard nothing Dad said?" Dominic reaches up and closes the casket, hiding Red beneath the maple wood. "Trust no one."

"So Slater though? You brought him into our family because—"

"I'm marrying his sister. That's family enough. Nick wasn't blood either, and—"

"My point exactly, Dominic." I turn and square off with him, puffing my chest out. "Nick had no allegiance to us because he was not blood. This Slater guy—"

"Knows I will kill anyone who crosses me." Dominic's finger pokes into my chest. "Including blood." His nostrils flare. "Now fall in line, Sven, because I don't want to attend another funeral for a family member."

His threat isn't even veiled. It's outright. He's telling me he will kill me without hesitation, the way the leader of this family should. Even my own father would take my life if it meant protecting the legacy. I nod, infuriated but not threatened. I know my place. And that place is to obey orders, even when I hate them. I back away, ramming a hand through my hair. I need a drink.

I head down to the pub where the family hangs out now and the—an old place called Al's on the corner a block away from where Allie used to work. I do my best thinking in this old bar. It's where I would come to toss a few back with Red when I needed advice, so it only seems fitting that I have a drink in his honor.

Tony, the bartender, jerks his chin upward as I enter, greeting me, and I slide onto an empty barstool between two other men whose faces are in their drinks. "The usual," I tell him, and he nods, heading off to pour my top-shelf Scotch. I nearly lost Tucker. David was severely injured. That bastard Paul is gunning for me now because I'm protecting his ex and kid. And now I have to deal with Jimmy Slater as my info guy—a man I know nothing about but already sense is not good for our family. The piece of crap put Red in danger. It's his fault Red is dead. How can Dominic not see that?

"How was the funeral?" Tony asks, sliding my glass in front of me. I reach into my wallet and pull out a twenty and toss it at him.

"Keep the change…" I pick up the drink and down it, then set it back down. "Fill it again, at least a double this time." I sigh, not really wanting to hash out the details of the funeral, but I know Tony was close with Red too. "It was real nice, Tony. Red would have liked it. Even my father spoke."

"Mmm, shame I had to miss it." He picks up the bottle of Scotch from the shelf behind himself and sets it on the bar next to my glass. "In Red's honor." He nudges it and bows at the shoulder, then walks away leaving me to my drink and a bit of peaceful introspection.

I began to think about how Red would handle Paul if he were here, what sort of things he would look up for me to find the man. I still have no clue where he is staying, though he seems to be a step ahead of me anyway. Even Red wasn't keeping up with Paul's movements. There is no way Slater will be any better at tracking Allie's ex. I toss back another drink, then another. And soon I'm feeling very drunk. It'll be a while before I can drive home, but stewing seems to be what my mind and body want right now.

Rubbing my face, I sit hunched over the bar, the near empty bottle of Scotch next to my empty glass. Ever since I laid eyes on Allie I knew I wanted her. It is a no-brainer for me that we belong together. The spark of connection looks different for each person—some people call that romance. I call it fate. She needs protection. I am a protector. Simple match made in heaven, and I plan to eliminate her need for protection soon, which will leave only desire. And I desire her a lot.

"Woah, buddy!" A man slams into my back, making me jolt so hard my arm thrusts into the bottle of Scotch and it takes a tumble, spilling out onto the floor. I lurch off my seat and come out swinging. I didn't even see who ran into me, but with two men already throwing punches, my fists fit right into the fray. I swing hard, connecting to one of their guts. The man doubles over and gasps, and I bring my knee up hard into his face.

"Fuck's sake, man. You broke his nose. We were just having a good time." The second man leans over the first, inspecting the stream of blood now trailing down to his chin and the first tears himself away, coming at me like a freight train.

He rams his shoulder into my gut and we tumble backward, slamming into the bar. I hear something crack in my back, and I bring my head down hard on his, headbutting him. He winces, throws a few punches, then backs away. Fists continue to fly, splintering bar stools and sending drinks toppling as other patrons scurry out of the way. And before I know it, I feel a strong pair of hands grabbing my shoulders from behind.

Rome stands in front of me, blocking my view of the bastards who interrupted my mourning, and I spin around to see Matty. He pulled me out of that fight and now he's glaring at me. "Tony called. What the fuck, Sven? Dom is going to have your head. Get the fuck out of here." He pushes me toward the door and I glare at the bleeding men as I am forced to retreat.

Matty pushes my shoulder again as I exit the pub, and I jerk away from him. "Keep your hands off me."

"What the hell were you thinking? On the day of Red's funeral?" He holds his hand out palm upward. "Keys."

I reach into my pocket and pull out my car keys and slap them on his palm as I open the car door. I would have killed those men if Matty and Rome hadn't interrupted me. As I sit down in the passenger seat of my car I notice Rome climbing into Matty's car. Being dragged home by my younger brother's isn't something I'm proud of, but at least I have a safe ride with a sober driver.

"You are impulsive and irrational. You're going to get yourself killed or thrown in the clink." Matty fires up the engine and pulls into traffic, headed toward my house. "Yeah, well you just need to let your inner demon out a little more. You have no idea how freeing it is to let loose." I really wish I had that last bit of Scotch which Tony is probably mopping off the floor right now. I'll have to remember to drop him some cash to replace the broken stools. It isn't the first time I've had to do that. Probably won't be the last. He was right to call my brothers.

"I thought Dom told you to grow up? You know he takes orders directly from Dad still." Matty cares too much what our father and brother think. He has yet to really break the need to please people. He would, someday.

"I thought you'd grow a pair too, but you haven't." I tug on the handle to lay the seat back and recline. My head is pounding, swirling with the sweet pungent whiskey. I may not show emotion like other men, but that doesn't mean I'm not grieving. Those punches were my tears. There will be many more like them before I get comfortable with the idea that Red is gone. Hopefully, some of them will land in Paul's face.

The car ride is silent, and Matty follows me into the house, giving the keys to Gerard—probably to make sure I don't head back into town and kick those guys' asses. As I'm sitting down on the sofa in my den, Allie walks in. I have no clue what my face looks like after bashing those two idiots around, but I feel it throbbing. She looks up at Matty and then at me, concerned.

"What happened?" she asks, tiptoeing past my brother. "You said you were going to a funeral."

Matty snorts and shakes his head. "Bar fight—after the funeral. Who are you?" He jerks his chin up and stares down his nose at her for a moment. "You're that woman from the diner."

"Allie," she says, but she only looks at me.

"Fuck off, Matty," I growl, and I can tell my words are slurred.

"Don't let him drive." Matty walks out and I hear the front door shut, and Allie crosses the room, scowling at me. Her petite form looks delicious. I'd like to have her, but given how much whiskey I've just drunk, I don't think I could stand, let alone fuck her. My eyes are heavy, blinking slowly as she hovers over me. She smells like strawberries in summer. I reach for her but she steps away.

"Your face looks awful." Her tone is not compassionate. It's accusatory. "You are bleeding again… You know, being here seems to be more dangerous than Paul ever was."

I try to stand, but at best I can only lean forward and plant my elbows on my knees as I endure her lecturing. I can't even blame her. She came into my life at a really shit time and she's seeing it at its worst.

"I don't feel safe here, Sven. I want to go back to my apartment before the landlord gives up the lease to someone else."

"You mean run? Don't you?" I ask, swaying. My eyes turn up to her face, but my vision is blurry. "Because you have no intention of staying around here with that nasty-ass ex of yours hunting you. Where will you vanish to this time? You know he'll just find you. I won't be there to protect you again. He'll kill you, you know? And he'll take Rico for real."

"Shut up!" she hisses. "He's twice the man you are. At least he never came home dripping in someone else's blood."

"Go to your room, now!" I stand, forcing myself to balance. "You agreed to this arrangement. Now just fucking do what I say."

She glares at me again, but doesn't argue, for which I am grateful, because the moment I sit back down, the alcohol gets the better of me, and I shut my eyes, fading into darkness.

15

ALLIE

Clutching the tea mug between my palms, I stare into Sarah's eyes. Sven allowed me to use his car and his butler to have a short visit with her, after me throwing a tantrum again. He insisted it wasn't safe, but when I told him Rico was staying at the house, he finally permitted it. Now I just want to feel better. My heart has been on a yoyo for days. Sven has truly done what he promised to do—protect me from Paul. But for every moment of feeling safe from my past, there has been a moment of feeling afraid for my future with Sven.

"But did you try to talk to him about it?" Sarah pries, sipping from her own cup. We aren't even drinking tea; it's just soda, but Sarah likes fine things, and thus the tea cups.

Her entire apartment is one fancy thing after another. She's modest, so nothing is too pricey, just in great taste. An old Victorian settee by the window, for example, which she purchased while thrifting for only five dollars. Then she recovered it with fake velvet and painted the worn-out wooden frame with gold spray paint. I love that old settee. It's things like that that make me wonder if people can change too, or if at their core they're just an old worn-out piece of furniture at risk of breaking beneath a heavy ass.

"That didn't go so well," I tell her, sipping my lime-green carbonated drink. It's not name brand—she's too frugal for that—but it's a drink. "Probably my fault for attacking him with my questions and accusations rather than talking, but I was afraid."

The old leather recliner squeaks as she reaches to set her cup on the table. I mimic her actions, setting mine down too. The glasses clink on the glass surface where rings remain from previous drinks whose sweat ran down and puddled as they warmed in the hot New York humidity.

"Look, so you don't know what he does for a living. He's never hurt you, has he? Never raised a fist to you, or struck you…" Sarah curls her legs up into the chair, sitting cross-legged like a child. I want to remind her to never sit like that, but I bite my tongue. She has no idea the toll that takes on her hips and lower back. She'll end up with surgery if she doesn't change her habits. Something my mother used to lecture me about, back when my mother cared.

"You hoo… Allie." She snaps her fingers in front of my face and I shake my head.

"No, he didn't hit me. I mean, once he grabbed my neck, but he stopped immediately and backed away. Sven isn't violent with me. And every time I've seen him interact with Rico, he's been about the most honest, real person I've ever seen. Rico really loves him." My shoulders droop. Sarah's question hit home.

"And he stopped Paul from getting Rico," she points out, literally. She points at me. I hate when she's right. I just feel powerless in Sven's home. I'm not used to this feeling. I've been running from Paul for so long, I gained independence. I hate being boxed in. I want my freedom, at the same time as enjoying safety.

"What's the harm in just trusting him?" Sarah drops her hand into her lap and shrugs. "Remember you can just file for divorce later on. Right now you're just feeling brave because you're untouchable. Paul can't get to you where you're at. If he was here in this apartment right now staring you down, would you still want to leave Sven? Would you still think Sven is more dangerous?"

"Ugh!" I growl. I cover my face with my hands and throw myself back into the chair. She's right and she knows it. "I hate this."

"You need him. Just ride it out until Paul is gone. Then decide if you still feel this way. You've been there like a week." I heard her slurp her teacup soda and then set the cup down again, and I lower my hands.

"He literally controls every move I make. I had to ask permission to come here." I know I'm whining but Sarah is my best friend. If she can't handle a bit of whining, I don't know where else to turn.

"But you're safe. Just think of it like having a body guard who knows things you don't." Then she wags her eyebrows at me. "And really fucking amazing sex to boot."

I snicker. She's got me there too. Sex with Sven is incredible. He makes me feel alive again, probably more alive than I've ever felt. And I don't think we've even tapped the surface of what he wants to do to me physically. Each time it's like a new adventure.

Her dryer buzzes and she pops to her feet. "Gott age the laundry out. Be right back." Sarah dashes off down the hall and I am alone with my thoughts. The only way I can fathom this working is if I have some semblance of my independent life. I need to go back to work, even if it's a risk. Maybe Sven will just send bodyguards or something, the way Sarah said.

I pull my phone out and call the diner, praying my manager is reasonable. I've missed four shifts without calling in at all. Dana has to miss me the way I miss her. I hold my breath as the line clicks and a voice comes across to my ear.

"Amelio's..."

"Hey, boss, it's Allie."

"Allie? Boss? You think you still have a job after not showing up all week?" he scoffs and I fully deserve that. I expect him to hang up, but he says, "What do you want? Your last paycheck?"

"Actually, I want to come back to work. I just had a lot of stuff going on. My ex came into town; my kid was kidnapped. It was this whole thing in the park. You probably saw it on the news." I bite my lip and wait for his response.

"I didn't watch the news. I'm sorry to hear that." His tone changes. He sounds more compassionate, and he's not known for being a compassionate man at all. He's a hard ass and pushes his employees to work harder for less pay than most places in town, but the likelihood of me finding a different job now is slim, especially with Sven micromanaging my existence.

"I swear, I didn't mean for this to happen. I will never let it happen again. I love this job. I can come back right away." I have no clue how to make that happen given the situation at home, but I know I have to. It is the only thing that will keep me sane.

"You know it's hard to find good help." The insinuated insult hurts but I let it roll off my back.

"I know. I swear I'm good help. You need me." I really try to sell it by pleading a little. "Please, I promise it won't happen again."

"Fine," he says, and I breathe a sigh of relief. "Show up at your normal shift tomorrow. Don't be late." He hangs up on me and I'm positively giddy as I shove my phone back into my pocket. Sarah returns, carrying a basket of laundry. She sets it on the settee and starts pulling things out one by one, folding it.

"Who was that?"

"My boss at the diner. He isn't going to fire me. I can go back to work." I stand and walk across the room to help her fold her towels. They are warm, and in this heat it's just added torture, but I'm antsy now, already trying to figure out how I will convince Sven to let me work.

"You think Sven's going to go for that?" She shakes a towel out, and a few strings fly off into the air, dropping to the basket beneath. Her hands deftly fold the blue cotton towel and I shrug.

"He has no choice. I'm going to be his wife, not his prisoner. It's just what is going to happen. I am going to put my foot down and make a way." And I will. Sven can't control me, at least, I don't think he can.

After finishing laundry with Sarah, I head back to the car, parked downstairs waiting on me, and I ask Gerard to take me home. He is polite and quiet. He treats me as if I have the same authority over him that Sven does, and it makes me wonder if I would have any luck ordering him to drive me to work or if Sven gave him orders not to do that. As we drive, I run through all the possible scenarios for how I could get to work and what excuses I can use with Sven to either persuade him to allow it or cover up what I'm really doing. If I lie, he'll probably find out, but it may be my only option. At least until he sees it's safe enough for me to do.

And every single cent I make now I can put into my bank and save up. Sven is paying for everything I need, and I have no other bills to speak of. It will be my rainy-day fund for when I inevitably leave Sven, because I just don't believe an arranged marriage is going to work for me. Not if I know nothing about the man I'm marrying and he refuses to tell me. In my mind it's settled. I save up by sneaking out to work until I have enough saved to get me and Rico away from this place for good.

When I walk through the door, Rico is there in the foyer, romping with Odin. The massive shepherd growls viciously like he wants to kill the boy, but he is only playing. Gerard snaps his fingers and the dog heels quickly, sitting back on his haunches and wagging his tail. Rico pops off the floor, covered in dog hair and a bit of drool, and grins like an idiot.

"Looks like someone is having too much fun. I have to take him out now. Excuse me, please." Gerard walks away and Odin follows obediently. The ball of fluff and fur is a lot more dog than I ever thought we'd have, but Rico loves him. He rushes up and wraps his arms around my waist.

"Hey, Mom. You have fun with Sarah?" He looks up at me and I see his face is pink from exertion. He looks hot, and I know I'm hot. I could go for a nice ice cold beverage or dish of ice cream.

"It was nice." I push his hair out of his eyes and then pinch his chin. "You have dog drool on your face."

"Odin likes to lick me," he says, grinning. "I'm hungry. Can we get a snack?"

"You read my mind." Nodding in the direction of the kitchen, I say, "How about ice cream or something?"

"Yes!" Rico cheers and races off toward the kitchen. He has really soaked in all the comforts of living in a very lavish home. When we leave, he's not going to be satisfied with the meager things I can supply for him. It breaks my heart that I can't give him the best things in life, but part of me is glad he has been so sheltered. Part of his adjusting to Sven's house so quickly has simply been the luxury of it all. He's never lived like this before.

I follow him into the kitchen where Marta is already reaching into the freezer to get a tub of ice cream, probably at the behest of my son. She winks at me and places the tub on the counter, then pulls out two bowls and spoons. I sit next to Rico at the table and take his hand. I know my news will be upsetting to him, but I hope it doesn't crush him.

"Baby, there is something I need to tell you."

119

He looks into my eyes with delight, completely unaware of what I'll say. He loves this place so much, and even Sven too, that I fear it will crush him.

"What?"

"Hey, I know you really like it here—"

"I always wanted a dog, Mom. This is awesome. Video games, a dog, my own room, and Sven is great too. He said he'd teach me how to play baseball if I want. Thanks, Mom, for bringing me here." My heart sinks into my chest, deflating my own excitement about what I see happening for my future.

"Bud, I know you love it, but we can't stay here." I glance at the maid who seems to not be paying attention. "I'm going back to work tomorrow. When I save up enough money, we are going to move, but this time we are moving far far away. I mean, maybe Chicago or Miami." I squeeze his chubby fingers but he pulls away.

"I don't want to. I really like Sven." He pouts and his brow furrows. "Why do you always do this? Why can't we stay in one place? And why can't I just be normal and see my dad like other kids?"

He is asking very challenging questions I don't have answers for. Not answers that he will understand anyway. I clench my jaw, reluctant to get into a deep discussion with Sven's maid standing over us. I don't know what she will report to him, or if she does, what he will say about it. The man is my only shield of defense against someone I know will kill me, so like it or not, I have to play nice, even if it means sneaking around behind his back just to make money to leave him.

"It's not fair," he says, crossing his arms over his chest. I hate when he is upset, and I knew this would upset him.

"Baby, it's just a lesson every person has to learn. Life isn't always fair. You just learn and move on." I reach for him again, but he pulls away.

As soon as Marta sets our ice cream in front of us, he picks up his bowl and spoon and says, "I'm eating this in my room." Then he promptly walks out. He's not disrespectful; I'd never allow that. But he is hurting, and I feel bad for being the cause of that pain. I watch him walk away, suddenly with no appetite for the creamy confection in front of me.

Marta leaves me to my thoughts, heading to the sink to wash up some dishes, and I stare at the bowl of Rocky Road. He doesn't understand now, but he will one day. I'm only trying to make a better life for him, protect him. I never had someone do this for me, and I know it's the right thing for him. Paul cannot get my son, and my gut tells me Sven —while protective and wealthy—just isn't the type of influence I want for my boy. What if Rico had seen the bleeding man or Sven come in beaten up? His questions would have topped mine, and he would be afraid too. I can't let that happen.

I'm saving up and leaving this place, even if Sven gets angry, even if Rico doesn't understand. It's what I have to do.

16

SVEN

Dominic's office smells like whiskey and sex. It's his wedding day and he couldn't keep it in his pants until after the ceremony—that or someone else was in here having a quickie. The chair I sit in stiffly faces him, his desk between us. He's furious with me. A man about to be married shouldn't have such a scowl on his face, but Dominic is the master of masking emotion. The second he walks out of this stuffy office into the garden to take his bride, he'll have a calm expression. Hell, he may even smile. I've seen the woman —Nanette—she's attractive. But she's no Allie.

"I just don't know what the hell you were thinking. Do you realize that three of the men you killed were loyal. I'm the only one who knows this right now, but if Dad catches wind—"

"He won't!" I snap, growling out my frustration. I know how stupid I was to open fire and march through that production floor without any intel. I don't need to be reminded. I was so angry over what happened with Paul, and the fact that Nick had just proven to be the mole; I wasn't thinking. "I've heard it all from Matty. I don't need another lecture."

"Sven, you're out of control." Dominic seethes, leaning forward and crossing his hands over his desk. His tuxedo coat wrinkles in front but he doesn't seem to care. "I can only cover up so much. Jimmy brought this to my attention this morning. You need to pull your head out of your ass and focus on your job. You have a family to protect, and I don't know why you insist on chasing a ghost."

"He's not a ghost. He is a threat to Allie." I reach up and loosen my tie. I hate ties, and I hate weddings. He's lucky I'm even here. I am wasting valuable time at this stupid even when I should be hunting down information. Even if Allie left, I'd still be hunting her ex. He played a sucker punch and I'll be damned if I let him get away with that.

"I get it that you like this woman, but you have to ask yourself if she is worth the distraction. It's costing us, Sven. And I don't like my people pulled away or distracted by trivial things. Let her sort this shit with her ex out on her own. Get your head in the game or you'll be benched."

"What is that supposed to mean?" I ask, standing to my feet.

Dominic's eyes say everything. He isn't playing. I can't fuck up anymore not for any reason. I never meant to make the mistakes I've made, and I never meant to let the family down either. I turn and shake my head, walking to the door. "Allie isn't just some woman, Dom. I'm going to marry her. Surely you get that." I wait for a second with my back to him, but he says nothing. So I walk into the hallway where I hear voices. The closer I get to them, the lower they get until they are hushed whispers. There is an intense conversation going on between Jimmy Slater and Allie. He clears his throat and looks up at me with professional tact as I approach, and I wonder what they were just discussing. To my knowledge Allie doesn't even know him, though I know almost as little about her as I allow her to know about me.

"Hello, Sven. Dominic said you may need my help with some things." Jimmy holds his hand out to me and I stare at it. Allie looks guilty, saucer eyes avoiding eye contact with me.

"Dominic is wrong." I grab her elbow and pull her closer to me and she tucks meekly into my side like she belongs there. Jimmy's eyes flick between her face and mine. "What were you two discussing?"

"The wedding—"

"The garden decorations—"

They both speak at once, and then Jimmy says, "The fact that the wedding is in the garden, and that Dominic's people did a fantastic job with the decorations." He adjusts his tie and takes a step back. "If you'll excuse me, I need to make sure Dom doesn't need anything before he marries my sister." He winks at Allie. "It was nice meeting you Ms. Clarke."

I wait for him to walk away and turn on her like a viper. "What was that about?" I hate the man anyway, but to see my future wife conspiring with him right under my nose is infuriating.

"Nothing. If you'd just answer my questions honestly I wouldn't have to go behind your back to ask people things that I should already know." She turns and walks toward the garden where other guests are already seated waiting for the wedding to start. Her pale floral dress sashays with her movement, swaying as her hips move back and forth provocatively. I follow behind her, frustrated but attracted. How does she make me feel so angry and so needy at the same time?

"Then fucking ask questions but don't be surprised if you don't like what you hear." I fall into step with her and drape her arm over mine so it looks like we're together. Heads turn as we make our way toward the family row near the front. Allie doesn't stop though. She speaks with a forced, tight smile on her face, out of the corner of her mouth.

"Are all of your relatives this rich? Or just you and your brother. This has something to do with what you do for a living?" Her tone isn't just anger; it's laced with fear too. She's right to fear my family and what I do for a living.

"You're in the business of criticizing how much money people have? Did it ever occur to you that my father is a wealthy man and raised us in that money?" It's true, though most of what I have I got on my own by hard work. Dad never gave us a cent. We had to earn our keep.

We sit, and the wedding begins. Her body is rigid, filled with all the questions she wants to ask but every time she opens her mouth I glare at her. During my brother's wedding is not the time to have this conversation.

Allie is an irritating woman at times, and today she is on my last nerve. When she tells me with conviction that she is going to work tonight, I instantly wonder what she's been doing the past several nights. She's been out with her friend Sarah, or that's what she has told me. I firmly grip her elbow and lead her away from the crowd of folks filtering into the dining room to feast and have cake.

"I already told you it's not safe," I hiss, leaning down to speak right into her ear. I can barely control my temper as it is, but she has a way of pushing my buttons that no one else ever could. She's my kryptonite, the thing that brings me to my knees. Outwardly, all I can express is anger, but inwardly I am feeling things for her. Things I haven't felt for a woman in years. Things that make a man weak if his enemies find out he feels them.

"I don't care, Sven. I want my freedom to live my life. Spouses are partners, not slaves. I want to have a job. I need interaction with people." She whimpers as I pull her into the alcove in the hallway outside the dining room. "Besides, we're not even married yet. I don't have to do everything you order me to do. I'm not a staff member."

Something rises up inside me at that moment that I can't control. I see the priest and then I see Tucker and I lose it. "You, and you—" I point at them and they look at me "—now." Jerking my head in a gesture meant to indicate I wanted them to follow me, I march Allie across the foyer to Dominic's office and she protests the whole way. She's already made it clear she isn't sure she wants to marry me, so rather than putting it off and allowing her more time to think about everything she's afraid of, I want to do it now.

"What are you doing?" she asks, spinning around as the priest and Tucker walk in. Tucker shuts the door after glancing to see if we were followed and I stare down at Allie's flustered face. Her cheeks are pink, matching the tint of her chest. She's flushed and it's incredibly sexy, but I'm not here to be aroused.

"Marry us now," I tell the priest with my eyes locked on Allie's.

"What!" she hisses.

"Sir, I'm not sure I can—"

I hear the grinding of metal as Tucker chambers a round and the priest stops short of finishing his sentence. "You have a hard time thinking that I can be a husband and provide for you everything you need. You insist you need your own job and human interaction, but you have no need of money. And I have more than enough staff for you to interact with. Fuck, start a garden club with Dominic's new wife. If you can't respect me now, then marry me now. Maybe then you'll respect me."

Allie backs away. Her hands are trembling, eyes flicking to the priest and then downward. "Sven…"

"You do as I say, or you get out of my house. Then who will protect you from Paul?" I am breathing down her neck, literally. I hover over her so close I can feel her shallow breathing on my face. I see fear in her eyes and I know it's fear of her ex, not me. I hate that I have to use fear as an ultimatum for her returned obedience, but she leaves me no choice.

"I can't imagine your brother will be happy with sharing his wedding anniversary." Her tone is changed, more docile, but she isn't truly complying with my wishes. I can see it in her eyes that she plans to rebel against me.

"Sir, if I may…" The priest's voice shakes with emotion. I turn over my shoulder to look at him. "I have to bless the food for Mr. Gusev." Tucker lowers his weapon and holsters it, and I nod at the priest who scurries away like a frightened cat.

"Leave us alone, Tuck." At my word, my right-hand man steps out of Dominic's office and I am alone with Allie. She slumps into a chair and buries her face in her hands, elbows planted firmly on her knees. "Allie, I'm doing my best to protect you, but if you don't listen to what I'm telling you, you're not going to be safe."

"I just want a normal life."

I pace, not even sure what a normal life is. My world isn't normal, despite living in the same city and breathing the same air. Allie doesn't get it. I've seen things that make grown men wet themselves. I've lived through things that changed me, shaped me into the killing machine this family needs—that Allie needs.

"I can't have you getting hurt. I can't allow it."

"Sven, please. I'm not getting hurt. Why can't you just send me a body-guard or something?" She stands and walks toward me and I face her.

"The answer is no."

She opens her mouth to speak and the door bursts open. Matty struts in grinning and his expression sobers. "I'm sorry. I didn't mean to interrupt." He holds up his hands defensively, probably because I'm glaring at him in anger.

"No interruption," Allie says, and walks toward the door. She is gone before I can stop her, and Matty continues his stride toward the liquor cabinet.

"What was that about? Dom asked for his good Scotch. I didn't mean to bust something up." He reaches into Dominic's cabinet and pulls out a bottle of warm brown liquor.

I don't even respond to him. I'm on the hunt, following Allie out the door and across the foyer. I have to keep her within arm's reach at all times. I don't mind if she learns my secret; I'd just rather have that on my terms, not because she is snooping.

17

ALLIE

I have been spending five nights a week out of the house and I can't even believe it's working. The first week I used Sarah as an excuse. Then at Dominic's wedding when Sven tried to rush the wedding plans, I realized he was probably on to me, or at least following me. So I got careful. I planned two nights at the library—I lied. Sarah met me in the back room and took Rico to her place and I snuck out the back entrance and went to work. When my three-hour shift was over, I walked back into the library and out the front with Rico, courtesy of Sarah once again. So far my plan is working.

Tonight I left Rico with the maid. I stand holding two dresses in hand, pretending to agonize over them. Dominic's goon, Tucker, hovers around me. His very conspicuous sunglasses indoors give him away as a bodyguard instantly, which is very cinematic, but I ignore the lame aesthetics of his look and focus on my plan to ditch him. I am not fond of either of the dresses, but I carry them both to the dressing room where men are not allowed and smile at the attendant.

She eyes me, then Tucker, then me again. "What can I do for you?" Her curt tone tells me she may not be the most helpful woman in the world, but I already have a plan in place for that too.

I glance over my shoulder, offering my most frightened expression when I turn back to her. Tucker stands wearing his dumb suit with his hands folded in front of himself and his back to me. I don't know why Sven makes them follow me around. I blame myself. If I had just kept my mouth shut about work, I'd be sneaking out to do whatever I want and he wouldn't be the wiser.

"I'd like a room please." I feign fear in my voice, talking timidly and keeping my voice quiet. Tucker doesn't turn around to see me, so that much is going right. She glances at my bodyguard again and her brow furrows. Then she picks up a key from the wall behind her where keys hang on hooks with numbers labeling them. "Follow me," she says, and this time her voice is quiet too. I follow her down a long row of doors all the way to the back. Another door along the wall—one that's different than the slotted wooden doors of the dressing rooms— looms in front of me. I know it's just the door to the warehouse that remains locked at all times because I worked here for about six months while hiding from Paul.

"Honey, is everything okay?" she asks, whispering over her shoulder.

"I could just use help getting away from him." I don't accuse him of anything or lie about him abusing me. I'm not stupid. I don't need the police sniffing around and making a mess for me now. That may draw Paul's attention. And all I want is to have a normal life. So if sneaking around and not telling Sven where I am gets me that then I will do it. Besides, my shift is only three hours again tonight. I can have Sarah give me a ride home and by the time Bozo Bodyguard figures out I'm gone, he'll have to search the entire department store for me before returning to tell Sven he's lost me.

"Is everything okay?" she hisses, pushing the key into the warehouse door. I knew it the moment she picked it up off the wall that she had gotten the warehouse door key. Door five. I used it a few times myself when a nursing mother needed a place to change her child's diaper, and once when a woman had to use the toilets. We weren't supposed to help, but people are still good. So I did. And this woman—Gretchen based on her nametag—must have a good heart too.

"It will be if I can just get away from him." I smile politely and hand her the dresses as I walk into the warehouse. She looks around anxiously and points at the back door. There are walls of shelves across the large room, stacked with boxes of all sorts of inventory. A tiny path marked by striped yellow tape shows the way down the walkway to the back door, which has a light above it indicating it is an exit.

"There, honey, you need me to call a cab?" Gretchen has kind eyes, and a motherly approach. I didn't peg her for this when I walked up to her, but I kinda like her.

"Thank you so much. I can call an Uber." I keep up my nervous act as I walk down the path I'd walked a hundred times toward the back door. When the warmth of the fading evening sun hits my face and the door slams shut behind me, I am home free. Just a four-block walk to the diner and I'll be at work.

I head down the alley to the street that runs perpendicular to the one the store is on. I have to stay a block south to avoid Tucker finding me when he walks out the front of the store to search. I'm warm, my clothing doubled up so I can wear my work uniform under a white blouse and black frilly skirt. I left my shoes at work two days ago, so when I get there at least I'll have something more comfortable than heels, but for now my feet ache.

My cigarettes are buried in my handbag beneath my wallet and cell phone. I pry my bag open with one hand—handles draped over my shoulder—and dig into the contents with the other until I find the cigarettes and lighter. I'm not a fiend, but I do enjoy a good smoke every now and then. I don't feel comfortable smoking at Sven's house. I have never thought it polite to smoke while in other people's homes or cars, so for the past few weeks I've been craving my smoke breaks.

Getting back to work a few days a week has helped calm my nerves for sure.

Traffic is light, only a few cars zipping past me, but foot traffic is normal for a New York city street. I keep my head down, avoiding eye contact with anyone as I slide one cigarette from the box and pinch it between my lips. The first drag after the flame catches is heaven. I suck in the thick smoke and fill my lungs, feeling the nicotine take the edge off my stress level instantly. It's a habit I should probably kick but some simple pleasures in life are essential, and this is mine.

Dana is standing out back waiting for me when I walk down the alley, finishing my cigarette. She squeals with delight and jumps up and down a few times. We've only worked three shifts together since I returned, so she's probably got some juicy gossip.

"O-m-g, you'll never believe who got promoted!" Her hand thrusts my shoes toward me and I drop my cigarette butt to the ground and stamp out the ember.

"Who?" I ask, blowing the smoke out. The wind carries it away as I take the shoes. Her fingernails are manicured, her lips slathered in thick, red lipstick. She's gorgeous and I'm jealous. I try to hide my own badly damaged manicure as I shed my heels and jam my sockless feet into the sneakers.

"Me!" Dana claps her hands and bends to snatch my heels into her hands as I bounce on one foot attempting to balance while tying my shoes. "Just yesterday. I'm assistant manager now, and the boss isn't here, so we are going to par-*tay*." Her exaggeration of the word party makes me chuckle. I can't tell she is happy about it.

I straighten and hand her my handbag so I can strip off the extra layer of clothing. "Congratulations. I'm really happy for you." It could have been me being promoted. I worked twice as hard and was never late, until Sven convinced me to just jet off with him. Now, I'm paying my dues. I can't be upset though. Dana deserves the promotion. "You get a raise too?" I peel the shirt off and hand it to her and she shoves it in my bag, juggling the heels in one hand.

"Two dollars an hour."

For two dollars an hour more I could be saving up so much faster, so I am upset with myself for not putting my foot down sooner. I missed those days and never even called in. "That's so good," I tell her, happy for her and jealous at the same time. I fiddle with the zipper on my skirt but it is snagged on the material underneath. My hands can't untangle it, so I turn. "Help," I tell her, and she shoves my bag and shoes back into my hands so she can manage the snagged zipper.

"This is a pain. I wish you didn't have to do this." After a few seconds of wrestling Dana frees me from the polyester trap and I slide it over my hips and carefully step out of it without letting it drag the ground in the alley.

"Can't leave this...." I pick up my cigarette butt, wishing for a little more time to have another, but it's time to start my shift. After shoving my skirt into the bag and tossing the butt into the bin, I follow Dana back inside where hungry customers are waiting on waitresses to fill their orders.

The shift goes about how a busy diner at supper time normally goes. The tips are crappy; I have bossy rude customers, and I am exhausted when it's over and I see Sarah's car pull up out front and park. As I'm leaving I snag my bag and shoes, kick off my sneakers in the manager's office, and start toward the front door, but Dana grabs my arm.

"I was so excited to tell you about the promotion that I forgot to tell you that that man came back looking for you again." Her eyes are serious and dark. She's concerned, so naturally my heart goes into fight or flight mode.

"What man?" Did Sven come asking about me? I was home though. Why would he ask about me when he knew I was home?

"Yeah, the creepy one you said was your ex. He hung around the back door all night. I had to call uniforms to chase him away."

I swallow hard. She's talking about Paul. He was here looking for me again, which means maybe I'm not as safe as I thought I was. "Thanks, Dana. I'll be safe."

My heart pounds in my chest as I walk out to Sarah's car and climb in. She is distracted by talking about some new person at her workplace who she loathes, so I change back into my street clothes and put my aching feet back into the heels. I feign calmness as she drives, though I could really use a cigarette or two—or ten. My hands shake as I button the blouse and by the time she drops me back at Sven's house, I'm in full-blown panic. Only then does she ask me what's wrong, but I tell her I have to go.

I can't let Sven be right. I can't show weakness, so why are my knees knocking and my stomach churning?

Inside, Sven is waiting for me. He stands with shoulders squared at the entrance to the bedroom, jaw set. "Hi," I mumble, hoping he doesn't look into my handbag where I stashed my dirty uniform that smells like greasy food. I stumble to the dresser and drop my bag, then kick off my heels. I'm exhausted and terrified. I don't have the mental energy to deal with a lecture.

"Where were you?" he asks sternly, and I know he knows I ditched Tucker.

"Well," I snap, spinning around. I'm the master of putting on an act when I need to. I've played this part a million times with Paul. It's more difficult with Sven, but it's what I have to do. Just a few more paychecks and I can start over. "If your ignorant, useless meat sack wouldn't walk off when I'm shopping, I'd have been home hours ago." I deflect, not answering his question in a direct lie—yet.

Sven takes a calm breath, studying my moves as I pull my earrings off and drop them on the dresser. "He said you went into the dressing room and never came out."

I scoff, turning my back as I unbutton my blouse so he can't read my expression as I lie to him. "If he wouldn't walk away when I'm changing, he wouldn't lose me. I looked around the store for twenty minutes, then I called Sarah. We went for coffee. Now can I shower in peace?"

My shirt slides down my arms and falls to the ground and I unzip the skirt, this time without getting the hanger caught. My eyes nervously flick toward the handbag where the work uniform is probably emitting an odor that will rat me out. He can't find that or I'm dead meat. I push the skirt over my hips, realizing I'm stripping in front of him. It gives me an idea—a way to make him forget about where I may or may not have been.

"Want to join me?" I ask, letting the skirt fall to the ground. Then I pull the pins out of my auburn hair and let it drape across my shoulders, falling from its messy French twist. He growls, and I know he's considering it. So when I unsnap my bra and remove it I know I've hooked him. The lacy material falls to the ground and my nipples harden against the chill of the air conditioning after having been drenched in sweat all evening. I don't turn to face him. Instead, I walk with authority to the bathroom and turn on the water, letting it get hot and steam the glass walls of the shower.

I sense him enter the room as I bend to remove my panties, and glance over my shoulder. There is a bulge in his pants and his hands are working to shed his clothing. With a half smirk, knowing I've gotten away with my scheme yet another day, I step into the shower and moments later he's there, crashing into me.

Sven's hands grope my body, fondling my tits and pinching my nipples before sliding between my legs and rubbing my clit. His lips cover mine in earnest, drinking in my kisses as the water rushes over our bodies. I'm not particularly in the mood for this after my stressful shift, but if it keeps him from suspecting me, I'll do what has to be done. Besides, his cock feels amazing and I don't mind an orgasm to take the edge off when I can't have a cigarette.

"You've been smoking," he growls, pinning me against the shower wall.

"You've been drinking," I counter. The hint of whiskey on his lips is sweet. Tempting.

I work my hand between our bodies, grabbing his cock and stroking it back and forth. He's so hard already, as if he were waiting for me to get home just to do this to me. It's flattering that he wants me like this.

"Tell me you've been thinking about me," he demands, gripping my wrists and pinning them above my head.

"I've been thinking about you," I say breathlessly, trying to match his growl.

"Good girl," he says, pushing my wet hair to the side and kissing my neck. I moan, even though it makes me feel dirty for enjoying it. I'm not a slut. I'm not. But I can pretend to be for him.

"I've been thinking about you all night," I tell him, arching my back against the cold tile wall.

"I'd like to hear about it," he says slowly.

"Well, I was thinking about how I wanted your cock in my mouth," I say in a low, sultry tone. "I wanted to suck you off until you came all over my face." I never thought that once, but he doesn't know that.

He groans, his cock twitching in my hand. "You've been a bad girl all night, haven't you?" Each time he contracts his muscles his dick dances. I squeeze it and stroke, drawing a bead of precum to his head.

"I'm sorry," I say. "I'll try to be better."

"I'll make you sorry," he says. He pulls his cock out of my hand and presses it against my wet slit, sliding it up and down until I'm begging for him to fuck me. Each time the head of his cock rubs against my clit I jolt with arousal. The water slicks our skin, making him glide between my thighs. It's torture; I want him in me.

"Please fuck me," I say. It's so much easier to say when I'm not looking him in the eyes. I'm not sure which is more demeaning, to beg him to fuck me or to look him in the eyes while I do it. Or maybe it's that I actually want him—when I initiated this just to get him off my back. Either way, his cock slides into me, filling me up and making me moan.

"Tell me what you were thinking when you were missing," he says, sliding in and out of me. His girth at this angle stretches my pussy and it's a glorious sensation. I moan in delight. His hands grip my hips masterfully, tilting my pelvis just slightly enough that his body rubs my clit as he thrusts.

"I was thinking about you," I say. "I was thinking about how I wanted to suck your cock off."

"That's right," he says, "you were thinking about sucking my cock off because you're mine."

I moan, pressing my back against the wall to steady myself. His words are getting me worked up, or maybe it's just his voice. Maybe I'm addicted to the way he talks to me.

"I'm yours," I moan. "I'm all yours."

"Oh yeah?" he says. "Tell me what you're mine for."

"I'm yours to fuck," I say.

"That's right. You're mine to fuck."

"I'm yours to fuck," I say again, "and you can do whatever you want with me." I claw at his skin, desperate to feel the waves of climax hit my body.

"That's right," he says. He picks up the pace, thrusting harder and harder, his cock sliding in and out of me. I can hear the sloshing of the water as it dances off our bodies and hits the floor. I lift my leg up and he hooks an arm beneath my knee, and I nearly come on the spot. The new angle is intense. "I can do whatever I want with you, can't I?"

I nod. I'm not sure I can speak. Whimpering has taken over my ability to speak.

"Say it," he says. "Tell me you're mine to do whatever I want with."

"I'm yours... to do... whatever you want with," I say quickly, panting between phrases. "I'm yours to do whatever you want with," I repeat. This time my voice is louder, desperate. I need him.

"Yeah?" he says.

"Yes," I say.

"You're mine to marry?" he growls, and I suck in a breath, clawing at his skin as my pussy clenches around his girth.

"You're mine to keep?" he says, and I moan as he slams his cock into me and I feel myself start to fall apart.

"You're mine to fuck?" he says, and I fall over the edge into orgasmic depths of pleasure and my body writhes and convulses in twitches against his, each spasm of my pussy sending another shockwave of pleasure through me. When his heat floods me I he grunts and bites down on my shoulder, not even bothering to move the soggy strands of hair. His teeth pinch my skin and I let out a yelp, but I'm too busy shuddering around him to make him stop.

I may have distracted him tonight from pressing the issue, but I don't think I'll be as lucky tomorrow. I need to be more careful. Maybe I need a better plan.

18

SVEN

I rinse myself off and give Allie a nice hard smack on the ass—hard enough to leave a handprint on her left butt cheek. She gasps then chuckles, turning her back on me, and I leave her there to shower. She's hiding something, using sex as a means to disguise her lies and deceptive behavior. If I weren't the one being lied to I'd be admittedly humbled by how good she is at the tactic. I dry off and dress as I marvel over how this woman is my perfect match and she doesn't even know it yet.

I was certain she'd blow a gasket when that priest said my last name last week, but Allie didn't bat an eyelash. Maybe the name Gusev means nothing to her. If so she's very far removed from the organized crime scene, which isn't a bad thing. It just means even more of a shock to her system when I finally explain who I am and what I do. I am simply waiting for a time to divulge my truth when it seems most appealing, the way my protection seems the lesser of two evils now.

Dressed and now on a mission, I head down to my office. On the way, I send Tucker a text to return to the office nestled in the far northwest corner of my home. He's already gotten an earful tonight from me about losing her in that department store, and after hearing her side, I know he isn't at fault for that. Now I have a new order for him. It's one I can do myself, but I'm proving a point to him. Dominic wants everyone vetted and despite my confidence in Tucker as my personal right-hand man, I have to test him.

He's there waiting for me when I walk in, though he has the sense to wait outside my door. "Boss," he says, opening the door for me. I brush past him and stroll right to my desk and flip on the lamp. The old tortoise shell Tiffany lamp illuminates the room which smells like leather and whiskey, two of my favorite things. I sit behind my desk and gesture to the empty chair across from me where Tucker takes a seat and crumples his hat in his hands.

"You fucked up today." I reach into my desk drawer, an old 1800's wooden block that weighs more than four hundred pounds. It took three large men to maneuver this contraption into this room but it has a civil war vibe I can't find anywhere else. I love it.

Tucker's head hangs in shame and his hands wring his hat tighter. "I'm sorry."

"I'm giving you a chance to redeem yourself." I take out the small tracking cookie and place it on the desk. My phone automatically connects to the signal when activated, so all I have to do is open the app and press a button and I'll know where this tiny little chip is at all times. I push it toward him and then sit back and he takes it. "Tomorrow, when you take Allie wherever it is she asks to go this time, you place that in her bag."

"Can't you just put it there tonight?" His question is a valid one. I can. Or he can do it for me. Besides, if she empties that bag and finds out I've planted something in there, she'll leave it behind.

"Do it. Then if she vanishes, just call me right away. It's that simple." I steeple my fingers across my stomach and he shrugs.

"Seems like an easy task, Sven. I don't get it." He sits straighter, some of the shame lifting from his tall, slender frame.

"Look, don't question me. Dominic wants people vetted. I trust you. This is your task. Do it well and we're on the up and up. Now get out. I have things to do."

Tucker stands and jams his hat back on his head before exiting my office. With Red gone and my only option for information being Jimmy "The Fuck-up" Slater, I have been forced to dig deep. I need to call a friend down at the station, someone on Dad's payroll I'd rather not deal with, but someone who can definitely help me. I don't want rollers figuring out what I'm up to, but I have no choice.

I pull my phone out and dial his number, one saved into my phone by default as a contact in case I'm in trouble. The guy used to be a beat cop but he's in anti-terrorism now and has access to some of the latest technology and police intel available. I just hate cops.

"Hello, this is Sergeant Monroe." Even his voice grates on my nerves, like fingernails on a chalkboard.

"Yeah, this is Gusev…" I let the name hit his ears for a few seconds before I continue. My name—my father's name—carries weight that people pay attention to. Apparently not Allie, but I enjoy her innocence of the matter right now.

"Dominic, nice to hear from you."

"Sven." I'm abrupt and I know it. I don't mess around with shit. "I need intel."

"Uh, yes, sorry. Mr. Gusev, I apologize for the confusion." I like how he squirms. It's entertaining. I may not be the Pakhan but I have authority and being the shoe hovering above a roach is a good feeling.

"Look, I need information on Paul Hensley and Allie Clarke. He's got a record; I know it. I just don't know what." I wait for him and hear movement in the background. It's late. I know he's not at work, but I don't care. When a man is on payroll with the Bratva they provide results when results are requested.

"One second," he mumbles, and I hear fumbling then typing. "Social security number? Driver's license?"

I grit my teeth. Of course I know nothing like that; I don't even know Allie's birthday. "All I know is they have a kid named Rico together."

After a few moments of silence I hear more typing and Monroe clears his throat. "Looks like he's got a DUI. No warrants, though he's tied to a couple domestics." There is more silence and then more typing. "She's got nothing except a few unpaid parking tickets from seven years ago. There is a note in her file about the doctors at multiple hospitals thinking her a victim of domestic abuse but she never filed a report."

Figures that Allie would be face to face with help and not take it. She really fears for her life with this bastard, which makes me want to get him all the more. "I need more on him. Anything you can use to hunt him down. I need to find him now."

"Sir," he says, more typing sounds in the background "Mr. Hensley is linked to an armed robbery and an attempted stabbing, but we never got the weapon to run ballistics. As for the stabbing, that happened only three weeks ago and the man is still recovering. He barely made it out of surgery. We are waiting for him to wake up so we can get a positive ID on the attacker. If it turns out to be Hensley we can—"

"Locations!" I snap. I don't have time for blubbering. I know this guy is a piece of trash that needs to be taken to the dump; I just need to know where to find him.

"The stabbing took place on the corner of Ninety-Fourth and Broadway. The attempted robbery within three blocks of that, Ninety-first and Amsterdam."

"Where does he live?" I take a deep breath, trying to calm my raging heart. This is why I need Red. He does this shit for me so I don't have to get so damn worked up. I drum my fingers on the desk while I wait for an answer.

"No known address, though the last known was six months ago on the lower east side."

"Get me more details. I'll call back tomorrow." I hang up before he can make excuses. Stewing over the fact that Paul is truly in the wind, I shove my phone into my pocket and stand up. I can't spend so much time trying to find him anymore. I need to get the shipping business back in line, which means hiring actual employees and vetting people to work in our armory. The two can't really overlap much because the temp agency frowns up on trying to source gun runners, and folks who want an honest job packing fish don't like bumping shoulders with the mob. It's a nightmare.

I shut off the lamp and head back to the bedroom. Allie will likely be in bed sleeping already, another tactic to avoid my questions. It's okay. I will just follow her tomorrow via the little tracking chip Tucker will place in her bag. I don't need to press her for information tonight. My suspicion is that she's sneaking out to work, which pisses me off, but she's not cheating at least. Still, I have to know. Dominic will slit my throat if Allie is a weak link.

When I pass through the foyer I see the lights still on in the game room, so I head up the stairs. Rico stares at the screen like a zombie, Odin on the couch next to him. Odin's tail flops around as I take a few steps into the room, but he lazily droops his head to the side as if to say he's not leaving his boy. I like that he's claimed Rico as his own. It feels fitting that my pet and Allie's son would bond.

"Hey, kid, it's late. You should be sleeping." I lean on the door frame and he blinks slowly and looks over at me. I can see the exhaustion in his eyes. He never leaves this room except to eat and half the time he takes his meals here.

"Mom already said that." Even his voice reveals fatigue. "Just one more game."

"I think now is good." I stroll over and take the controller from his reluctant hands and he yawns. "I know you like these things but your

143

eyes are going to go bad if you keep staring at a screen all day every single day."

Rico stands up and stretches. "I took Odin out to the backyard to play earlier. I wasn't on the game the whole day." He walks past me, his fingers tapping his side, and Odin leaps off the couch and follows him into the hallway. I flip off the television and trail behind him, shutting off the lights as we exit the game room.

"Can Jordan come over and play? He will like the games. I never got to invite him to our apartment because he always wants to play video games and I don't have my own game." Rico's stockinged feet shuffle on the slick floors. More and more he reminds me of myself, and I find my heart actually craving fatherhood. I'd have never thought I'd want something so normal, so non-mob related, but I do.

"Sure, we can work that out I think." I follow him to his room and he rests his hand on the doorknob.

"Can Odin sleep with me? I know Gerard always makes him sleep downstairs, but he likes me." His sleepy eyes and disheveled hair are cute. I can't resist him.

"Sure, just leave your door open in case he needs to sneak out the back to use a tree." I push his door open and give Odin the signal to enter. He's a well-trained guard dog, but I can see Rico is bringing out his protective nurturing side too. He's all too happy to leap onto Rico's bed. "Good night, kid."

"Hey, Sven?" Rico says, pulling his shirt off. He uses it to rub his eyes and then blinks up at me with tired eyes.

"Yeah?" I linger in the doorway for a second.

"Thanks for letting me stay here. I like it. I think Mom likes it too. I just want her to want to stay."

"I want her to too, kid. Goodnight."

By the time I get down the stairs to my room, I'm ready for sleep too. I enter the room and I am right. Allie is either very adept at pretending to sleep, or she's forced herself to shut down just to avoid me. I strip off and slide into bed next to her. When I do, I reach for her, pulling her against my chest. She's still naked, her body still moist from the shower. She is actually sleeping.

Work must have been exhausting for her, and I wish things weren't the way they are. I'd like to have heard about her day, celebrated her victories and mourned her losses with her. I just don't know how to send her out into this world where only horrible things await her.

As I hold her, I think of my mother. She killed herself. I didn't see any of it, not the blood or even her room afterward. Dominic took the brunt of that psychological trauma for the family. But I know how I felt when she was just gone. She was here; then she wasn't. I'm not letting that happen to me again. Allie is mine, and though I don't understand why she has become the cornerstone of my heart, she has. She just has to fucking listen to me so I can keep her safe. Because if that bastard kills her, or even harms a hair on her head, I'm not coming back from it this time.

Dominic thinks I'm a little out of control now? How will he feel when I go *John Rambo* on this city and take out every last vestige of rage I have over Allie Clarke being threatened or harmed?

19

ALLIE

The way Sarah eats her fries is ridiculous, dipping them into her chocolate shake. We sit at the picnic table behind the diner to have dinner since Sarah has the night off. We've not had an actual chance to hang out in a few days since I've been working, and since she is my excuse to leave the house most days, I feel like I need to spend time with her to ease my guilty conscience.

"That's so gross," I tell her, eating my fries the normal way, with ketchup. She snickers and shrugs, chewing her concoction in peace. It's a warm night. The fries and shakes hit the spot, but I still have an hour of work left before thinking up a good excuse as to who I've been with and why I ditched Tucker earlier tonight at the grocery store. I wanted to use Sarah as an excuse again, go to her house for a few hours before coming to work, then sneaking back over before Tucker picked me up, but Sven asked me to linger with him longer this afternoon. I had no good reason to avoid interacting with him, and by the time I got out of there, Sarah was already at her work shift down the street. I was forced to lie and say I needed tampons and that Tucker had to drive me to the store.

"What are you thinking?" she asks, having another ice-cream covered French fry. I sigh and dust the salty grease off my fingers.

"I'm sick of sneaking around. I want this to be my real life without having to lie. I mean, Sven is okay. The sex is good. He mostly lets me do what I want around the house. I'm saving up enough that as long as things are going well I can be out of here in just a few more weeks, but the stress is starting to mount up." I crumple the fry container and throw it in the bin behind me then pick up my shake and slurp it out of the straw.

"What do you mean?" Sarah's fries are almost gone, which means she will have to go back to work soon. And that means I will have to go back to work soon and finish my shift. I'm not prepared with a logical excuse tonight. I just knew if I didn't show up to work I'd be fired.

"I mean, last night Sven almost caught me in my lie. I ducked out of Gimbels and came to work and left his guard there. When I got back, I had to use sex as a distraction to keep him from asking me things I'd have to lie about. I'm a horrible liar. He knows it too."

Sarah snickers and wags her eyebrows. "So how was it?" Of course she wants to know details about my sexual exploits because she's not getting any herself.

"Don't get me wrong, shower sex is amazing." I snicker and continue. "But I don't want to feel guilty about lying."

"Then don't feel guilty. Just do what you have to do." She shrugs her shoulder and tosses her trash into the bin. "What is the harm in that?"

"I don't know. I just feel like Sven may be more dangerous than either of us realize." I bite my lip. I know I've been over this with her before and she told me to give him a chance, but I'm still not comfortable with not knowing about him. Things don't add up.

"I told you. He's never laid a hand on you. Doesn't that mean something? Paul beat the hell out of you and tried to kidnap your kid" She stands, brushing her slacks off, and picks up her drink.

147

Something needles at my conscience. At the wedding, I felt like I was so close to getting some answers from Sven, but when I pushed the wrong button, he got irrational, pushy even. I can see he has an impulse control problem and a lot of built-up anger. I don't know enough about him to rationalize away his defense mechanisms like some women might. Maybe he was abused or maybe he watched his brother get shot or something. I don't know. What I do know is he has some issues.

What I also know is that he's secretive. The only thing I know about him is what I learned from a priest. His last name is Gusev, at least if my logic follows. His brother was called "Mr. Gusev" by the priest, so it stands to reason that Sven shares the same last name, and that might be a clue to finding out what I'm actually getting into.

"What is it?" Sarah asks, hovering. I know she only has a few minutes left, but she knows this city better than me. Maybe she knows of any significance to the name.

"So I overheard the priest at Sven's brother's wedding call him Mr. Gusev." I look up at her face and sigh. There is a fleeting look of terror and she licks her lip. "Do you know anything about the Gusevs?"

She sinks back onto the picnic table and glances at the door of the diner, propped open with a brick so I can get back in. She leans in close, her voice low. "Girl, you think Sven is a Gusev?"

My heart flutters and races. "Is that a bad thing?" I ask, now licking my lips. I want another drink of my shake in order to make my throat not feel like I swallowed a cotton ball.

"Uh, you've never heard of the Gusev Crime Family? Girl, they're the biggest organized crime syndicate in the city. Bratva... Russians?" Sarah acts like I'm stupid for not knowing this, but I have never heard a thing about it. When I was younger I just focused on my life, fashion, school, dating boys. And after Paul, the only thing I can do is run. Life never gave me a chance to slow down and pay attention to the news or things happening in the city.

"No..." I can't believe that. I refuse to believe that I am living under the roof of a notorious criminal. "I mean Sven wouldn't—"

"Stop. Listen to yourself. His name is Sven. That's pretty Russian sounding. Right?" She stands again and backs away a step. "I have to get to work. If I had known who this guy is from the beginning I'd never have encouraged this. You need to get away from him fast, girl. You come stay at my place. Bring Rico. I have a space in my attic that he can use for a room. We'll have to get an air conditioner up there, but with the cold front moving through later it will probably be cool for a few days."

"Wait, Sarah!" I call, standing, but she keeps backing away.

"I'm going to be late. I'm just saying, please take my advice. Come stay with me." Then she's gone, turned around the corner to hustle back to work, and I'm left standing with an empty shake container and a dry mouth.

I toss the container and shudder in fright as I walk back into the diner. I don't want to believe that Sven is that man, that his family is that family, but I know it adds up. The bleeding man, his fight in the bar, the way his cousin was murdered, the fact that the priest was trembling before him and his bodyguard pulled a gun without even so much as a whisper of an order. I rake my hand through my hair and find myself ice cold, anxiety setting in.

Paul is deadly. I know that. But so is Sven, probably worse. My gut has been right the whole time. I need to be away from him; I just don't know how to do it and keep Rico safe at the same time. Sven offers me protection I need in exchange for the most amazing sex I could ever ask for. It's not a bad exchange until you factor in that I'm going to marry a mobster.

"Something wrong?" Dana asks when I walk in. "You're white as a ghost."

149

"No… N-nothing," I stutter, staring down at the trays of food plated up and ready to be served.

"Good, this goes to table four. This one to eight. I need you out there." Dana pushes a tray toward me and picks up her own and I am left trembling as I stare at the food.

My mind is a swirl of confusion. Over the past few weeks I've really adjusted to life with Sven. We've had our differences, sure, but I'm comfortable. I've felt safer with him in this short time than I have felt in a decade. It's not just the sex either. His commanding presence puts me at ease. I'm not afraid of him—or anyone else when I'm with him. No man has ever made me feel like that. I like that feeling.

But the mob? The Bratva? He's one of them? And how can I reconcile raising my son into that family? Rico deserves a life that isn't one of bloodshed and crime. I don't want my baby boy growing up a gang member getting shot at and killing people. I can't do it. He needs freedom to be whatever he wants and Sven's family is dangerous.

But Paul—god. If Paul gets ahold of Rico, the only life Rico will have is running from police, drugs, and whores. And who's to say Paul won't kill me and abuse Rico in the process. He's not a good person. He belongs behind bars; he just hasn't been caught for the things he's done. I'm on the verge of tears when Dana bursts back into the kitchen with a scowl on her face.

"Allie, just because we're friends doesn't mean you can slack off. I'm your boss now. You have to get to work!" Her tone is anger laced with a bit of whining. I blink away the tears and pick up the tray, balancing it on my shoulder. Then I back up to the swinging door and head out to the dining room. Dana shouldn't even be waiting tables, which shows me how much she wants to help out. I've been slacking for too long. I try to push away my emotion and work, but as the last plate of food off my tray is set in front of a customer, I see Sven walk in with Tucker. He's angry.

I tuck my tray under my arm and notice Dana eye me with a nasty look. "I'm sorry," I mouth as she passes me.

"Two minutes, that's it." Her shoulder bumps into mine and I nearly drop the tray, but I clamber to secure it and move toward him.

"Let's sit down," he says, but I plant my feet by the host stand.

"I can't," I hiss. "I'm on the clock." Tucker glares at me as he backs out the door and Sven grips my elbow so tightly I know it will leave a bruise.

"I didn't ask." He forces me into a booth and I lay my tray on the table. The red leather squeaks as we sit. I'm really uncomfortable, but I find myself strangely calm—not at all afraid, even knowing who he is now.

"I know who you are," I blurt out. "I know who your family is."

His eyebrows rise. I expect him to rage, to be angry and scream. He doesn't even raise his voice.

"Then you know how I am able to protect you." His firm gaze holds me captive, searching my heart to its depths. There is compassion there, well masked. A man like Sven doesn't show emotion or empathy, or love. But when I look there, I can actually see it, which makes what I have to say even more difficult.

"So you had me followed?" I am irritated, but not surprised. I knew it was coming.

"Tracked actually, a bug in your handbag." He draws his tongue across his teeth and then sighs. "Look, Allie, I'm just trying to protect you like you asked. I want a wife; you want safety. It's a win-win." He folds his hands in front of himself and leans across the table. He's about to say something when Dana walks up.

"I need you to get back to work, Allie. And you, you need to leave." She picks up the empty tray and glares at Sven, who opens the front of his coat and flashes a weapon. Again, no surprise there. Now that it has all clicked in my head, nothing he does shocks me. He's used to getting his way because he owns this town.

"Get out or I'm calling the cops." Dana stomps off and I whimper.

"I need this job, Sven. I have to get back to work." My palms are sweating. People are staring. They probably know who this guy is and I have been so blind this whole time.

"You don't need to work, Allie. I'll take care of everything you need."

I stand, straightening my skirt. "You don't get it, do you? I left Paul because he did shit like your family does. I don't want to raise my son around criminals. I can't accept your protection anymore. I'm going to stay with Sarah."

He stands too, now the pain in his eyes trickles out onto his forehead where deep crevices form, and to his lips that pucker into an angry glare. I am still not afraid of him. He will never hurt me. To him I am a prized possession, worth more than all the gold in the world. I can see it in the way he looks at me.

"You can't mean that."

A siren in the distance wails and I tense. "You better go."

"I'll drive you home when you are done."

Sven ducks out of the diner and I do the walk of shame back to the dining room to finish my shift. I know I'll be in for a lecture when I get home but at least I've made my position clear. Even if it is breaking my heart. Why does leaving Sven hurt? Why does it feel like he meant something to me? He meant nothing to me—just sex and protection. Right?

"Snap out of it, Allie. Get back to work." Dana is now being heartless, and I understand why. Now my job really hangs in the balance. I need to have these last paychecks and get out of town for real. Paul isn't safe. Sven isn't safe. And if they aren't, neither is Rico.

20

SVEN

I can't believe she's so insolent. I stand between her and her suitcase after driving her home and she refuses to listen to me. "Get out of the way, Sven." She sidesteps, but I do too, blocking her.

"You're not leaving." She can't. I won't let her. This is her home now. I should have made the priest go through with it, marry us on the spot. My heart is racing, rage pushing my pulse skyward.

"Get out of my way and let me pack. I already told you it's over." She steps around me and opens the suitcase, piling an armful of clothing into it. My insistence and demands aren't working. If she doesn't change her mind I will be forced to physically prevent her from leaving, which I swore I wouldn't do. I won't be physical with her like that bastard.

"Okay, fine you can work. I'll send a bodyguard with you." If this is what she wants then I will use it to my advantage. I will send Tucker, let her do her shifts at the diner. Maybe it will draw Paul into the open and I'll get my chance at him. God knows if Monroe doesn't find him first, he's going to hurt someone else. I need to take drastic measures.

"No. I appreciate the attempt; I just can't do it. My son deserves better." She returns to the dresser and I realize how much she has settled in. Another armful of the clothing purchased for her and it doesn't fit in her suitcase.

"Mom?" Rico's voice from the doorway stops us both in our tracks. We've been shouting at each other and he looks afraid. "Are you okay? Why are you angry?" His bottom lip trembles and Allie rushes over to him, hugging his head to her stomach.

"Oh, baby, I'm not angry. Okay?" Her hands frame his face and she makes him look up at her. "We're going to stay at Sarah's place for a few days, okay? Go put your things in a bag."

"What? No. I like it here," he protests, backing up. "Sven, make her stop."

My heart clenches. I remember what it's like to feel that feeling, sadness and love. I was a boy with a heart full of emotion and compassion once. Now I'm a killing machine. It's all I know. I know orders and respect, retribution and victory. I can't respond to him. All I can do is stare at a mother hugging her son whose heart is hurting.

"Go on, pack now." She nudges him out the door and he pleads with me.

"Sven, please. I don't want to leave. I like it here." Rico cries, giant crocodile tears streaming down his cheeks.

"Go on, respect your mother." I sigh, still believing I can stop this all from happening. If nothing else, I am going to murder that bastard Hensley and convince Allie she needs me still. I don't know how, but I will. "Take anything you want from the game room."

Allie glances at me, relief in her eyes. "Yeah, anything you want. Now go pack up." She nudges him again and he stomps out, sobbing. I am completely enraged that she would make her son feel like this when he clearly wants to be here. That rage bubbles over into my body and I clench my hands into fists. But the moment she shuts the door and turns to me with compassion in her eyes, I soften too.

"Thank you. I know this is hard on him. I appreciate your kindness."

"Kindness? That wasn't kindness. That was respect. I offer it to you because that's how I live my life."

She stands by the door, her hand still resting on the knob. "Men like you don't understand women like me. Sven, I can't raise my son around the violence."

"Twenty-two counts of sexual battery."

Her eyebrows furrow at my words. "What?"

"Three charges for attempted murder. Seven different IDs in seven different states."

"What are you talking about, Sven? Is this your record? Are you confessing to me now who you really are so that I'll stay? You think telling me your secrets now is going to change anything?" Allie shakes her head and walks toward the suitcase, folds the lid shut and starts to zip it. My next words freeze her in place.

"Paul Marcus Davenport, a.k.a. Paul Hensley. He's a killer, a rapist, and a con artist, Allie. He's dangerous. I talked to the cop downtown who is set to serve an arrest warrant. I had Tucker give the sergeant a lock of Rico's hair from his hairbrush. Paul's DNA is linked to horrible crimes."

She turns to face me, her face drained of color. "I can't raise my son with you, Sven."

"Then at least stay until they catch him." My lip wants to tremble, but I can't understand why. All I want is her safe.

"I can't. I need to go to Sarah's." Allie's eyes fill with tears. She takes a deep breath and breathes it out slowly. "I care about you, Sven. You got into my head so much that I fucking love you now. And being with you one more night when I know who you are, when I know I can't stay with you, well that's going to fuck my heart up more than Paul's fists ever fucked up my face." She blinks and tears stream down her cheeks.

"Stay..." I ask her again, but she resolutely shakes her head.

I cup her cheek and pull her closer. "I can't," she whispers.

"I need you here." Something comes over me. Something I haven't felt in years, decades maybe. "I want you here."

"You can't have me, Sven. My son comes first. I need him safe now."

She doesn't resist when I lean down and kiss her, our lips brushing lightly over each other. "I can keep you safe."

"Can you keep us safe from your family? From random men who come into your home bleeding? From people like the ones who murdered your cousin? From—"

I kiss her again, holding her head firmly. My life is a fucking warzone. I walk across situations just waiting for landmines to explode and claim my life every day. I'm a killer and a heathen and she is everything pure and right about this world. She's right. Being around me isn't safe. But I'm not safe without her. I'm not ever going to be safe without her. I kiss her again, as if it is the last time I will ever see her. Knowing her ex, it may damn well be.

"Sven," she whimpers, crying into my mouth. Her words protest my advances, but her hands grip my biceps.

"Allie, please don't leave." As our lips meet, I feel a fire ignite inside of me. A fire that I can't quench. Allie may not be safe with me, but I know one thing for sure—I can't let her go. Not now, not ever. This is temporary; just until Paul comes out of hiding.

I grab her by the backs of the thighs and lift her, spreading her legs. She wraps them around my waist as she clings to my shoulders. The scent of her arousal wafts up between us, and I know she wants me. She's light as a feather in my arms.

I carry her to the bed and lay her down, gazing at her with a fierce intensity. My heart pounds with a raw, desperate need for her. She looks up at me, her eyes wide and vulnerable, and I know I can't hold back anymore. I open the fly of my pants, pulling out my shaft, and climb onto the bed, hovering over her. I trail kisses down her neck, reveling in the softness of her skin. Allie moans, arching her back as I reach for her breasts, cupping them in my hands through the fabric of her shirt. Her nipples harden under my touch, and I push the neckline of her top and bra down and take a nipple into my mouth, sucking and biting gently.

She writhes beneath me, her fingers digging into my back. I move down her body, kissing and licking each centimeter of skin I can expose on my way to her core. I hate this damn work uniform. I have to really work to pull her top up, just to nip at her side and hip. Allie gasps as I spread her legs, and pull her panties to the side, then part her folds, my tongue flicking over her clit. She tastes sweet and salty, and I can't get enough of her.

I bury my face between her thighs, devouring her with long, slow strokes. She cries out, her body writhing with pleasure. I keep going, lost in the sensation of her, and slide a few fingers into her abyss. She's perfect in every way. I want to remember this moment. My fingers thrust into her, pleasuring her, and her hands lace through my hair.

"Sven," she moans, guttural growls escaping as I suck her clit. I want to hear her screaming my name. I want to feel her come around my fingers, her walls clenching around me. I need to possess her completely. Her thighs press against the sides of my head, squeezing it. Her hips rise up to meet me, grinding her pussy on my face and I growl at the way it makes me feel hungrier for her.

I plunge my fingers into her, and she comes apart beneath me, crying out my name. I roll my tongue over her clit as she throbs around me, and her body shakes. "God, Sven," she whispers, her breath coming in jagged gasps. She reaches down to pull me up, and I climb over her, kissing her hungrily, ready to taste her again. Allie's a work of art, her curves are perfect, her breasts round and full, her hips made to cradle me. Her legs are toned and tanned, and as she wraps them around me, her thighs quiver. My slacks slide over her muscles, each muscle tensing with desire. She moans, and her lips are red and swollen.

The musky scent of sex is in the air, and as I slide my cock inside her, the smell of her arousal makes me ache with need. She moans into my mouth, and I push forward as she arches her back, giving me full access. Each stroke makes her wetter and wetter until my cock slides in and out of her with ease. Her legs tighten around my waist, her ankles locked at my back. I can't get deep enough; I want to be a part of her. I want to keep her here with me forever.

The only thing in my mind, as I entered her, was how much I want her, how getting inside her to the very core of her is all that matters. And as I sink into her the world explodes into a blur of color behind my eyelids. She's tight and wet around me, like velvet over adamant. Her strong muscles squeeze me, milking me, and I thrust harder.

Allie wraps her arms around me, her fingernails digging into my shirt. I pull her up so I can see her face, my cock buried inside her. She's so beautiful, flooding my senses, and I have to have her. I hold her against my chest and move faster, thrusting into soft and willing warmth. My movements become erratic, and I know I'm close. I can feel my balls drawing up, a tight pressure building.

"Oh God, Sven, I'm going to come again," she murmurs. The sound of her voice, the feeling of her body under mine, the scent of her skin, her hair, the taste of her lips, all of it makes my head spin. She's like a drug, and I'm so high on her that I never want to come down.

"I'm going to come too," I moan.

"Do it, come in me," she whispers, and her words send me over the edge. I pump into her a couple more times, and I come with a growl, my hips jerking involuntarily. I'm still inside her when she comes too, her walls fluttering around me as her head falls back. Her body spasms and shudders beneath me.

Allie's gorgeous in the throes of passion, her cheeks flushed, her lips swollen, her eyes smoky and lust filled. The sounds she makes, like she's trying to hold in screams, are heaven to my ears.

My entire body is shaking, and my vision is blurry. I've never come so hard in my life, and I'm still hard. Allie is still writhing under me, her legs still wrapped around me. Her pussy is so tight around my cock that I don't ever want to leave. I bury my face in her neck, breathing her in, inhaling her scent. She smells like sex and lemons and the ocean. I can't get enough of it.

"Stay," I prompt her one last time, but her sniffles tell me I am not getting my way, not this time, not with her.

I pull out, feeling the scratch of her panties along my cock as I slowly retreat from her body. Then I offer her my hand. She stands and fixes her panties, grimacing at the cum on her fingers. When she returns from washing her hands in the bathroom, she heads right to her suitcase and attempts to zip it. I zip my cock away inside my pants and use my knee on the top of the bulging luggage so she can close it.

"Thank you for taking such good care of us. And thank you for protecting me." Her glistening eyes hide so many fears that I want to remove from her permanently, but she's not actually mine. I wanted her to be. I need her to be. But she is choosing to walk away.

"Stay," I say again, knowing she won't, but giving orders is the only thing I'm good at.

"Drive me to Sarah's?" she asks, and my heart sinks. I nod, reluctantly agreeing to something I do not want. "I'm going to check on Rico."

She rises up on her tiptoes and kisses my cheek. It's bittersweet as I watch her walk out the door.

I hoist her suitcase off the bed and follow her to the door. When she turns to head upstairs, I head for the front door and leave the suitcase. I tried soft and romantic once, with Lacy. I was a different man back then, before cancer stole her the way suicide stole my mother. I don't feel emotion now. It's better that way. I'm less irrational, more controlled. Or am I? Because being around Allie has made me laser focused, and nothing in my world will seem right anymore.

I stand staring at the bottom step as if I can change her mind. As if some word I can think up to speak to her will make me not be a murderer or Bratva member. But Bratva blood runs deep in my veins. It's my life. It's everything I have ever known, everything I am. To change that would be to change into someone I am not, someone she doesn't love. She admitted her love, so why can't I acknowledge that she might be important to me other than giving her orders?

"Ready?" she asks, carrying Rico's suitcase. His face is drawn. He holds an Xbox and some wires in his hand.

"No." I am firm, but I won't force her to stay. It has to be her choice. I won't make her a slave.

"Mom, please?" Rico pleads one last time, but she looks away from him toward the door.

I hate goodbyes.

21

ALLIE

Sven loads my things into the car as Rico clings to Odin's neck. The poor beast doesn't know what's happening, but Rico's heart is broken. I'm certain if Sarah's building manager would allow her to have a dog, Sven would send Odin along just to make Rico smile. As it is, the gaming equipment will take up too much room.

"Ready?" I ask him, and he sulks to the car, dragging his feet. He doesn't understand how difficult of a situation this is for me too. I follow behind him slowly, knowing I'm walking out of the lap of luxury into a life of working hard and running. Sven was the best thing that ever happened to me until I realized I jumped out of the frying pan and into the fryer.

Sven holds the door open for Rico who climbs in and buckles himself. Then he opens my door. "You don't have to do this." His eyes plead with me to stay, but I've already told him enough times.

"I do," I tell him as I climb in and reach for the seat belt. Sven shuts the door and gets in the driver's seat. He says nothing as he drives us across town to Sarah's apartment. I have to point it out to him, which makes me realize maybe he wasn't stalking me as much as I thought he was in the beginning. Some of my harsh feelings about his line of work make me doubt myself now, what I'm doing. Sven never laid a hand on me—he wouldn't. I actually care about him too, in a way I never did with Paul. I just wish he wasn't a part of something so violent and dangerous.

"Want me to carry your things up?" he asks, pulling into a parking space on the street and putting his car in park. I glance at the building. Sarah's place is on the top floor and there is no elevator. It's only three stories, but it's a heavy bag.

"No," I tell him, unbuckling my things. I will have to carry my bag and Rico's while Rico carries his video games. "I'll be fine." I open the door and climb out, and Sven is there, opening Rico's door. I didn't realize he even cared about my son so much. I never really saw them interact, though I also know nothing about the way he was raised or the way his father treated him. For all I know this could have been the epitome of love for a man born to the Bratva.

"Mom, I don't want to stay at Sarah's. I don't have a good feeling." Rico's chocolate eyes stare up at me. I wonder if he's just using a line I've given him or if his gut is telling him something mine isn't telling me. We stand facing each other as his bottom lip quivers while Sven gets our bags out of the trunk.

"Baby, this is for the best, okay. You'll see." I tousle his hair, but now my gut is churning. Sven has been my source of comfort and safety for the past few weeks and I know for a fact that Paul was looking for me at the diner this week. If I'm making the wrong choice and I don't even know it, I'm not sure how to swallow my pride and turn around.

"Here," Sven says, setting the suitcases next to me on the sidewalk. "If you change your mind, you have my number."

"Sven, tell her she's wrong," Rico pleads, and Sven crouches in front of him. He pushes some stray hair out of Rico's eyes and then pinches his chin.

"Respect your mother, okay. She loves you a lot, and she will do anything to make sure you're safe."

"But—"

"That's an order," Sven tells my boy and I'm not sure what has transpired between them previous to this conversation, but Rico nods his head tightly.

"Yes, sir." Rico's shoulders are slumped as he walks toward the door of the building. I pick up the suitcases, not quite ready to shut the door to this chapter of my life. I just wish things were different, that Sven's life wasn't so… criminal, for lack of a better word.

"Goodbye, Sven…"

"It's Stephen." His tone is calm and even. "Stephen Victor Gusev, son of Alexsi Roman Gusev, Pakhan of the Bratva, but you knew most of that already." He puffs out his chest and gazes at me. I can see the pain and longing in his eyes, but there is also pride there, ego too. "I cannot change my blood. I can't change my family, or my job, or the men around me who I call brothers. I'm sorry that this didn't work out."

If this is his way of saying he loves me or that he's heartbroken, he has a long way to go before he touches my emotions. I nod at him and walk away. I'm feeling my heart being torn from my chest and I can't turn around to look at him, not even when I hear the car doors shut and the engine start up.

It's a long trek to the third floor, but we make it to Sarah's door, a little winded and tired, but in one piece. Sarah welcomes us in. It's late, and I'm ready to collapse, but we have to get Rico settled first, so she leads us through a small closet in her second bedroom, into a door and a narrow staircase. It's dark and musty, but we get to the attic space of the old rental building and Sarah flips on a light.

"This is my bedroom?" Rico asks, looking around the cramped room. Boxes line the walls, cobwebs in the corners everywhere. There is a small window open, the sound of thunder rolling in the distance. The cold front will come, bringing with it a breeze to cool the hot space off.

"Yep, all for you." Sarah pats his shoulder and moves toward a tiny twin-size bed along the wall near the window. "I have a TV we can get set up for your Xbox tomorrow. It's kinda late for games tonight."

"Mom," he whines, turning to me.

"She's right, bud. Sleep tonight. We have plenty of time for video games tomorrow." I leave his bag near the bed and run a hand through my hair. It isn't the Ritz but it's home, and it's far away from my old apartment where I know Paul would find us within minutes. "Sven will have the rest of your things brought over here tomorrow, okay?"

"Fine," he pouts, setting his gaming console down on a box. "Just let me sleep." Rico kicks off his shoes and tosses himself on the bed. Sarah looks at me as if to ask if everything is okay, then heads for the door. I don't like that Rico is upset, but I'm not sure how to calm him.

"Bud, you know I love you, right?" I touch his back lightly, worried about him.

"I know." He buries his face in his pillow. He just needs space.

"I'm going downstairs. If you need anything you come get me."

I straighten and walk to the top of the narrow stairs. When I look back at him he's curled on his side facing away from me. I flip off the light and descend the stairs, squeezing out of the closet and into my room. It's modest, a full-size bed against one wall, a dresser on another. There is no window, but I had no windows in my old apartment either. I take a few minutes and hang some of my dresses in the closet so they don't wrinkle too badly, and Sarah appears in the doorway with a bottle of wine and two glasses.

"Want to vent?" she asks, head cocked to the side.

"Girl, you read my mind." My heart is heavy as we walk out to the living room and I curl up on her sofa. Lightning flashes outside, thunder rumbling over the city. Sarah uncorks the wine and pours two glasses full and sits next to me. She already has a box of tissues and a few chocolates laid out on the table. She knows me too well.

"You're doing the right thing, Allie." As she sits on the squeaky couch she hands me one of the glasses and I indulge myself right away. God I wish she would let me smoke a cigarette too.

"I wish I felt that way." I set my glass to the side and hug my knees to my chest. "I feel like I'm hurting Rico left and right. He wants to know his father, but Paul is off limits. So we get all set up with Sven, who Rico seems to love, and then I have to take that away too." The audible confession drives nails into my metaphoric coffin. "I feel like a horrible mother."

"And that's not all," Sarah says, sipping her wine.

"What?"

"You actually like that guy." Her expression of sympathy makes me want to cry, but I refuse. I've cried enough tears over men in my life; I have to be strong this time. I shrug, ignoring her comment.

"It's the right thing. You said so yourself."

"But you love him?" Her question scalds my heart. I do love him, but it doesn't matter. A mother's love for her son trumps any romantic love out there. I have to protect Rico with my life.

"It's the right thing." I pick up the wine and finish the glass in two swallows. I want to drown what I'm feeling for Sven, with hope that maybe tomorrow I wake up and pretend this never happened, that I don't feel a thing for him anymore.

"Well, I have chocolates and ice cream. We can watch a chick flick and even pin Paul's picture to my dartboard and practice throwing darts."

She snickers and pushes the tissues toward me. "And it's okay to cry and be upset about this. I'm sorry I encouraged you to go for him. I should have known it was something fucked up like this." Her apology is genuine, but unnecessary. I'm an adult. I make my own choices and this is all on me.

"It's okay... But maybe I'll take you up on that ice cream. With as uncertain as my future is right now, I will take anything I can get to help myself stay calm." I uncurl my legs and turn, stretching my feet out to prop them on the coffee table. My legs are sore from walking around at work and I just want to melt into this sofa and forget life.

"Sure, I'll go dish up a few bowls." Sarah stands to walk to the kitchen, but as she does, someone knocks on the door. She glances at me with confusion. "Forget something in Sven's car?" she asks, brow furrowed.

I think about it for a second. I have my purse in my suitcase, phone in my pocket, and Rico brought everything he wanted in his bag. "I don't think so." This is her apartment, not mine. Why would someone come knocking for me?

"Hm..." she mutters and heads for the door. She looks through the peephole and backs away quickly. "Uh... Allie—" As she says my name the door opens. I jump off the couch, bumping into the table. The wine bottle wobbles and terror claws at my neck and chest. Paul walks in with a gun pointed at Sarah.

"Where is she?" he asks her before looking up to see me.

Sarah squeals and runs over to me, wrapping her arms around me. "Get out of my house."

"Paul, what are you doing here? Put the gun down." I hold my hands up, surrendering. "There's no need for a gun. Sarah is just letting me sleep over." My thoughts go immediately to Rico tucked away safely in the attic. I pray he is sleeping now, that he won't hear any of what happens.

"Where is my boy, Allie?"

"What do you mean?" I ask as he starts looking around the room. He shuts the front door, then opens the coat closet on the adjacent wall.

"My son, Rico. Where is he? He's mine and I want to see him." Paul is glassy-eyed, a crazed look on his face. He's high on something; I just don't know what. Sarah's arms squeeze me so tight I can't move. She's whimpering, but I can't even tell her Paul will respond negatively to that. I have to be the strong one again, stand up to him.

"He's not here."

"Bullshit!" Paul screams, whipping the gun around to point it at me. In all the times he was abusive to me, he never used a weapon. This is terrifying. I might piss myself. "I watched you both come into the building—followed you from that rich bastard's house." He advances on me and Sarah grips me more tightly.

"He's not here," I say firmly, praying he doesn't get loud and startle Rico. The boy will just come down here and Paul will get violent with me. "He's at a friend's house in a different apartment."

"Bull fucking shit!" Paul darts off down the hallway, stepping into Sarah's bedroom first. I pry myself out of Sarah's arms to follow him and she whines.

"Call 9-1-1," I hiss then race down the hall.

In Sarah's room, Paul throws open the closet door and tosses a few things around, then heads for the bathroom door. He's on a warpath I'd rather not be on with him, but my life may very well hang in the balance.

"I told you he's not here," I snap, trying to move him away from the bathroom. All the evidence that Rico even exists is in that attic. I have to keep Paul away from the closet in my room or he will see the door.

"Get out of my way," he says, using the pistol to smack me across the face. I yelp in pain, covering my cheek and cower for a moment. He

167

moves back to the door and down the hall, opening the laundry closet. I follow him, now feeling terror prickling my skin. There is nowhere for Rico to hide in the laundry, so Paul moves on to the last door—my room.

"Paul, he isn't here! You're violating Sarah's space." I grab his arm, trying to prevent him from going into my room, but he shoves me hard against the wall. My body slams into the old plaster and I knock my head hard. "Ow..." I wince, taking a moment to steady myself after the blow.

He walks into my room boldly, turning my suitcase out as if Rico could hide in it. He spins around an angry look on his face, then notices the closet door. "Paul, give it a fucking rest. He's not here," I snap, but this time fear glues my feet to the old wooden planks.

Paul opens the closet door, and shakes his head. The way my dresses hang blocks the view to the door behind them. He spins around and grabs me by the neck, forcing me out into the hallway. While terror stiffens every muscle in my body, adrenaline preparing me for a fight, relief washes over me. He hasn't seen the attic door. As long as Rico stays in his room he'll be safe.

"Which apartment?" he hisses, shoving me forward as soon as we enter the living room. Sarah is gone, the front door standing open. I can't blame her for running. I'd have run too if my son wasn't here.

"I'm not telling you, you sick bastard." I stumble and fall to my knees. It feels like I'm going to throw up. Paul heads for the door, gun in hand. "What do you think you're going to do? Hold up every tenant in this building? The cops will be here before you get downstairs."

"You're right. I'll just take you. Your friend will cough up the kid, or you die." Paul grabs me by the hair, yanking me to my feet. I hold in the shout of pain that wants to escape so that I don't alert Rico to the danger, and move with Paul wherever he leads.

Rico is safe.

Rico won't be harmed.

I repeat the phrases in my head over and over as Paul leads me to God knows where.

Rico is safe…

22

SVEN

The home already feels empty, not like a home. I didn't realize how much I adjusted to Allie and Rico being here until she was gone. Odin sits at my feet whimpering. Even he knows it's not right. I'm furious with her because she knows better, but she is just the sort of woman who has to learn the hard way.

The bottle of Jameson sits on the table next to my feet unopened. I have a glass for it; I just don't have emotional energy to open it and drink it. I keep replaying every detail I know about Paul Hensley in my head, hoping something will click and I'll figure out where he is. Now more than ever I want that bastard dead, for no other reason than I've been hunting him for weeks now and I've not been success- ful. This rage inside of me has to go somewhere, and I intend to make sure it goes directly into his body, fists or bullets—it's all the same to me.

Odin's ears perk and a low growl rumbles out of his chest. He hears something I don't, but I'm not even put on edge. No one would dare mess with me in this state. I remain reclined on the sofa, but I watch the hallway floor just outside my door. A shadow passes by and a few moments later I see Matty's frame enter the doorway. His face is expressionless, but his poor posture reveals his mood. He stops a few strides into the room and Odin rests his chin on his paws.

"I got news about Pop."

"Yeah?" I ask, still not sitting up. Let life kick me in the balls while I'm down. I come back twice as strong anyway.

"They're putting him on hospice." Matty moves into the room farther, sitting in one of the arm chairs across the table from me. Hospice isn't good. It's basically saying they've given up hope and they're just making him comfortable now. "He's officially signed all the documents needed to transfer everything to Dom."

Matty eyes my Jameson then looks up at me. I say nothing, but I give him permission with my eyes. "When did this happen?" I ask. I'm not surprised by the news. At Red's funeral he was in bad shape. He can barely walk as it is. His ability to swallow and talk at times is so poor he has to be fed via an IV.

"Just a while ago. I told Dom I'd fill you in. Looks like another funeral soon." Matty cracks the seal on the Jameson and pours a few fingers into the glass. "Want some?" he asks, pausing before he takes a sip.

"In a bit..." I sit straighter, placing my feet on the floor. Just because I knew my father was getting worse doesn't make it any easier to adjust to the idea that he won't be here one day. Death is the inevitable end of every life. It's to be expected not feared. It's what my father has told me a thousand times. Thinking this way—that death is just the final phase of life for all creatures—is supposed to remove the pain of it. It evaporates a lot of the pain of someone you care for being taken from you and makes it easier to move on.

But Allie isn't dead. She just walked away.

"What's wrong with you?" he asks, then empties the glass of its contents.

171

Forcing Allie to stay when she clearly didn't want to be here would have been wrong, so I let her go. With Dad I'm not getting that choice. He goes whether I want him to or not. I need to get over there and visit him before he's so far gone with the drugs that he can't communicate with me.

"Nothing," I mumble, then stand and walk to my liquor cabinet. I pull out another glass and return to the sofa and Matty pours me a drink.

"You heard Dom got that bastard who was shorting us? He's dead." Matty sips his drink, talking shop like he didn't just tell me our family structure is getting its overhaul even as we speak. Dominic will go all balls to the wall with his attitude and authority for a while to prove he's the real leader. It means putting up with his ego and anger issues for a while too. I hate that, but it's the way it is. I nod at Matty. I hadn't heard that, but it's good. I failed at doing my job. At least Dominic was able to fix it.

"And he hired a new foreman for the factory today. I thought you were doing that?"

I take the glass as he slides it across the table toward me. The Jameson sloshes in the glass. It has a scent like no other whiskey, calming me before I've even had a single sip. I lift it to my lips and finish the glass in one drink. I didn't know Dominic took that over either. I've been so distracted with my personal shit, hunting Paul, trying to watch Allie, that my mind has been scatterbrained. I know it will only get worse until I get her out of my system.

"I didn't." I set the glass back down and he refills it. I don't need that much more yet, so I let it sit there and stare into the swirling honey colored liquid.

"Yeah, I think Dom's pissed at you to say the least."

This entire conversation is wearing on me. I don't want to talk shop. I don't want to hear what Dominic is saying or doing. I don't want to know my father is dying or that the company is getting new management. I want to let the caged lion loose to hunt. My temper has been bottled up too long and Paul Hensley is the target I'm aiming at.

Usually Matty and I get along well no matter what. But tonight, I just want him to leave.

"Oh and Jimmy is working out okay. He's the guy who made the hit on—"

"Shut up, Matty."

"What? I thought you'd want to know the guy hunting Red for so long is dead." Matty scowls at me. "You're still pissed I didn't make the hit myself?"

What I'm pissed about is far more complex than even I know, but hearing the name of Jimmy Slater in conjunction with my failure just sets me off.

"Get out," I say gruffly.

Matty huffs and sets his empty glass down. "Pull your head out of your ass, Sven. Slater is here to stay. You can't just—"

"Get out!" I roar, picking up my glass and throwing it against the wall. It smashes to a thousand shards and Matty scowls at me before retreating. Nothing is going the way it's supposed to, and I'm the sort of guy who gets what he wants. I don't quit. I don't let my enemies off the hook, and I don't let someone walk away. What the hell is wrong with me?

I grip handfuls of my hair and rest my elbows on my knees. I know Dominic is right. I'm out of control and even the tiny bit of control I felt when I had a focus—keeping Allie safe—is gone. All I can think about is slitting that bastard's throat and then making her see how she's made a mistake. She and I belong together.

My phone rings. I'm raging, my chest heaving, so I ignore it. I'm in no mood for a social call, and work can fuck off. I pick up the Jameson and skip the glass this time, swigging it straight from the bottle. And my phone rings again. It's not a social call; I know that much. Which means it's either a family matter or business. I don't care about either. I ignore it again, standing and striding out the door and heading toward my room. I carry the Jameson with me. I'm going to need it.

The bedroom light is off, but I leave it that way. I turn my ringer off and toss my phone onto the nightstand and set the Jameson next to it. I am seated on the edge of the bed, unbuttoning my shirt, when my phone lights up. It's yet another call, but this time I can see who is calling. It's not work or family–it's Monroe. Why the hell is he calling me?

My instinct says I need to answer, so I do.

"What is it?" I bark.

"Sir, I've got a huge lead on that guy you're hunting."

My body tenses, a jolt of energy zipping through my muscles. "What is it?" I ask him, already buttoning my shirt up again.

"Since this guy has so many counts against him and an active arrest warrant, they have a BOLO out. I have a few friends in Vice who have been keeping tabs on things and there was a 9-1-1 call made from Manhattan twenty minutes ago. Paul Hensley's name came across the scanner. He abducted a woman from her friend's apartment at gunpoint, left her kid behind."

My worst nightmare is coming true. I stand, supercharged for this fight. He isn't taking her. Not on my watch, not like this. "Where is he? Do they have a bead on his location?"

"Get this, the address Vice says they need to search based on witness testimony is only two blocks away. It's like this guy set up shop by the friend's place hoping she came around there." Monroe sounds chuffed with himself to have figured this out but all I can think is how much of an idiot he is. Jimmy Slater may have figured this out faster.

"Send me an address now." I hang up on the sergeant and immediately call Allie's phone. If she has it, maybe she'll answer. If not, maybe Sarah will pick up.

I grab my keys and the gun out of my nightstand drawer and pinch my phone between my ear and shoulder as I head out toward the car. The phone rings and rings, no answer. I jam the gun into my waistband and climb into my car. Then I dial again.

I feel my phone buzz, probably the address sent by Monroe, so when the call doesn't go through again, I end it and type the address into my GPS, then call again. After seven tries, someone picks up.

"Hello?" It's Rico's scared voice. "Sven?"

"Hey, buddy. Yeah it's me." I am definitely not a nurturer but I try to remain calm, despite my thirst for blood at this exact moment. "Tell me what happened."

"Sven, where's my mom? Sarah said some bad man took her. There are police here."

"Buddy, where was your mom's phone?" I pull out onto the road and floor the accelerator. GPS says it's a fifteen minute drive. I intend to do it in seven.

"It was under the couch. Sven, the police say I can't stay with Sarah. They said I have to go with them." Rico sounds terrified. Who the hell would do that to a kid? Sarah is his nanny.

"Let me talk to Sarah."

"Okay," he mumbles, and I hear him sniffle. There is some talking; I hear male voices in the background and think I recognize one. Then I heard Rico pleading with Sarah and the phone crackles.

"Yeah," she snaps. She's not happy to talk to me.

"Sarah, it's Sven. Tell me what the fuck happened." I turn down a side street and the GPS screams at me to turn around, but this way is faster. I know the traffic will be lighter here.

"He fucking took her, you bastard. Why did you get her into this shit? She'd have been gone by now, somewhere safe."

So she blames me. That's fine. When I come in as the hero, she will change her tune. "Did he say where he was taking her? Why?"

"He wants Rico. We hid him, so Paul didn't know where he was." Sarah sniffles too. God, so many people crying.

"I'm coming." My gruff nature doesn't allow for me to sound comforting right now.

"What good can you do now? They're taking Rico to the station and then to DHS. They don't know where she is either."

"I'm going to get her back. You tell whoever it is in your home that they need to talk to Sergeant Monroe in anti terrorism. He'll make sure you get to keep Rico. Got that?"

"What?" she asks, her tone softening.

"Tell him Sven Gusev needs a favor." I hang up knowing she will be in good hands now, and hit the talk to text button. The phone chimes. "Send Monroe a text."

"Okay, what would you like to say?" The computer talks to me as my car bumps over a rough patch of road.

"The kid stays with the nanny."

"Okay, your text says, 'The kid stays with the nanny.' Would you like to send it?"

"Yes."

The swooshing sound of a message being sent echoes out in my car speakers and I check the GPS. Only a few blocks away now. He better not have laid a hand on her or I will make his death slow and painful.

23

ALLIE

I can't tell where we are. The room is dark and I've been crying too much so my vision is blurry. It's an apartment of some kind, though it is in a horrible state of disrepair. The walls are filthy, covered in handprints, dirt, and mold. The carpet looks like someone vomited on it and left it to dry. It smells like rotting garbage and sewage. He can't possibly be living here. But there is a single mattress on the floor in the corner of the room with a dirty sheet draped over it, so maybe he is.

I'm seated on a chair in the corner of the room where he left me. My hands are tied behind my back, my feet zip-tied to the legs of the chair. Paul paces the room, gun in hand. He keeps running his hand through his hair like a lunatic. I don't see any drugs or paraphernalia but I know he's not sober. Something is eating away at him and it's not just the fact that I'm hiding his son from him.

"Where is he, Allie? Where is my boy?"

"Fuck you," I say, then I spit at his feet. I won't give Rico up. I'd sooner go back to Sven and let the Bratva raise my son. No, I've come this far in trying to give Rico a better life. I can't cave in just because I'm afraid. Sarah called 9-1-1; I know she did. When we were in that shitbox of a car headed away from Sarah's apartment, I heard sirens.

Paul is angry. He stomps over and uses the back of his hand to strike my face. He hits the same spot where he pistol whipped me earlier and I yelp in pain. Tears fill my eyes and leak out against my will. I don't want him to see me cry, but it's painful.

"Tell me where he is." Paul hovers over me, demanding answers I won't give him. He'll have to kill me first and even then, the court will lock him up. He'll never have Rico.

I can't respond. My face hurts too badly. My head hangs and I taste blood on my tongue. I see his shoes move away from me across the room and I let my eyes shut briefly. Everything in my body hurts, my shoulders, knees, every joint. I don't remember ever getting a beating this bad, but he's got me. I know he won't let me go unless I give him what he wants and even then he may still kill me. My silence protects my son, and he can't force me to talk.

"My god," he hisses and finally he leaves the room, walking into an adjacent room.

My neck hurts as I lift my head. I struggle against the rope tying my wrists together but all I manage to do is give myself rug burn. Rico must be terrified. And Sarah—I know they won't let him stay with her. I need to get to him, and that sudden need to comfort my son causes me to struggle against the restraint harder. My entire life the past ten years has been devoted to loving that little boy with everything inside of me. I have to fight harder. I can't let Paul get to me.

But what if I can manage to get Paul to change his mind? Paul is on something; he's not thinking straight. I've seen him like this before. I remember a night when he was so drunk and high on something that I was able to calm him down so he didn't hit me, just by offering him sex. I used that tactic on Sven, hoping to get information that night. I know it will work. I just have to convince him that I'm being sincere with him.

I'm ready when he walks back into the room. This time the gun is tucked in his waistband and he has a beer in his hand. His angry glower hasn't softened any at all, but I'm practiced at helping change his mood. I have done this for years; I just have to dig into my memories to remember important things about how to calm him. Admittedly it would be easier if I were free and not tied to a chair, but my words will have to do.

"Paul, please let me go. I know we can work this out." I lick the coppery tasting liquid off my lip and stare him in the eye. "Baby, I'm sorry that I've been away. I just got selfish. I—"

"Shut up," he hisses, then slurps his beer. I don't think that drinking is a good thing for him right now because of whatever else he's taken, but if I warn him, he'll just get upset with me again.

"Look, let me help you relax, okay? We can connect and talk about our future." Paul stops pacing and moves closer to me. I hope I'm getting through. If this works and I get through to him, all I have to do is get him to drink so much he passes out and then I can escape. "Baby, I'm so sorry. I shouldn't have left you. You were right for me and you deserve to see Rico."

He snarls as I say his son's name, but I press on. "He misses you. He asks about you sometimes. You'd love him. He's smart and funny. He loves video games and superheroes. And he's got a dog. Its name is Odin." Now I'm just lying, but it seems to be calming him down. He sways, taking another swig of his beer as he hovers over me. His expression is growing softer. "He gets all As in school. He's so smart. And he wants to play soccer. I will sign him up in the fall, I think. You like soccer."

"You expect me to buy this shit?" he asks, then he brings the beer bottle to his lips again and drinks the rest. When he's finished, he smashes it on the ground and shakes his head at me. My heart sinks.

"I mean it, Paul. I mean everything I said. Rico really misses you. He asked about you just yesterday. And I—"

"You," he snarls, glaring at me, "have kept me from my son for years. You are a piece of garbage I want out of my life for good. You have no intention of letting me be with my son. This is just more of your manipulation to make me let you go so you can escape. I know your game, Allie, so stop playing. Just tell me where he is."

Anger starts to rise up again but I push it back down. My wrists are burning; I want out of these restraints. "I'm not manipulating you. I am telling you I realize that I am better off with you. Sven was violent —really violent." The words are bitter on my tongue. Sven would never hurt me. I hate saying this about him. "He kills people a lot. He comes home covered in blood."

Paul stalks closer, his boot crunching the broken bottle. "You think that's violent? You don't even know what violence is, honey."

The stench of alcohol on his breath makes me gag and tears well up in my eyes. Paul laughs a deep, hearty laugh and uses my hair to pull my head upward so I'm forced to look at him. "I know you hate me. I can see it in your eyes. You detest me. You want to get away from here."

"No, baby," I mewl, forcing the bile down my throat. "I want to reconnect." If my hands were free I would touch him, as disgusting as that sounds. I just want to put him at ease so he'll let me out.

Paul holds my head up with a tight grip on my hair and smacks me across the face with the other hand. He has no intention of letting me out. I can't hold back the tears anymore. I'm terrified now. He's sick, and I'm afraid he's going to hurt me really badly this time.

"Paul, please," I plead, sobbing and gasping for breath. My chest hurts more now, shoulders too. I try again in vain to free myself from the rope binding my wrists.

"You know, you're a waste of breath. Maybe I'll just wait 'til the cops clear out and then I'll go back to that apartment and take your little friend. She will tell me where my son is." Paul drops my head and my body stiffens, sending a jolt of pain down my spine.

"No, Paul, leave Sarah out of this." I lift my head again only to see the back of his hand come down toward my face.

"Please," I whimper, but the blow nearly knocks me and the chair over. At the same time I hear a loud crash. I don't hit the floor, but something booms around me. I'm crying so hard again I can barely see, but someone has busted the door in. I blink hard, and look up, using my shoulder to try to dry my eyes. The only thing that does is make my neck and face hurt more.

"Sven!" He's here? And he's angry. He stands with hands turned to fists just inside the door he smashed open.

"You sick fuck," he says, moving with stealth and speed. He rams a shoulder into Paul's gut and they slam into the wall. Paul is surprised, his eyebrows high. He pushes back, forcing Sven away from his body, but Sven comes back at him with a punch to the face.

"Sven!" I fight to get my hands free. I feel the ropes loosening up, but my skin is on fire. I may even be bleeding. "Sven, he has a gun." I try to warn him as Paul starts to fight back. Fists are flying everywhere. Paul fights dirty too. When Sven knocks him down, Paul grabs a handful of the broken glass. He rises back up, using the hand with the glass in it to swipe at Sven's face.

"Bastard, get the fuck out of my apartment." Paul charges at Sven again, and this time it's Sven's turn to take a gut shot. Paul's head connects hard with Sven's gut, knocking the wind out of him and the gun out of his waistband. Paul spots it as Sven is bent over trying to catch his breath.

"Sven! Oh my god!" I yank at the restraints now as Paul dives to the floor. Hand lands only inches from the gun and Sven sees what he's doing too. As he sucks in a breath, Sven dives on top of Paul. His hand doesn't reach the gun either, and they wrestle across the filthy carpet.

My mind races with terror. I tug and tug on the restraints, sobbing hard. They're in an all-out brawl to get to the gun first, and I'm tied to this chair. If Paul gets it, he'll kill Sven and then me. I can't let that happen.

"Please, Paul..." I plead, but they are so focused on their fight, I know he can't hear me.

Paul forces Sven off of himself by rolling, then slams Sven's head against the wall. Sven closes his eyes briefly. It looks like he's dizzy. In that split second, Paul gets the gun and chambers a round. The metal-on-metal sound snaps Sven out of his daze and just as Paul aims the weapon, Sven grabs his wrist. The gun goes off, blasting a hole in the wall just over Sven's shoulder.

He lurches forward with Paul's wrist in hand and knocks him backward to the floor.

"Holy fuck..." This is bad. I glance at the door. No one is coming to save either of us. I don't know where this apartment is or if there are other people in this building or not. Someone has to have heard that shot. I tug at the rope, feeling it loosen even more now.

Sven, now on top of Paul, has the advantage. I watch them spit and cuss at each other as Sven tries to get the gun out of Paul's hand. They roll across the carpet, besting one another until Paul is victorious, using all of his body weight to pin Sven down. The gun is hidden between their bodies somewhere, and both of their faces are red with exertion.

"You're going to die tonight, for what you did to her, and from what you took from me." Sven's brow furrows in concentration.

"Sven! Please, be careful," I shout, pulling at the rope. I feel it give way just as the gun goes off. "No!" I scream, scrambling to free myself from the now-loose ropes. Paul lays across Sven's chest, head down, and Sven's eyes are shut. Blood pours out of one of them, pooling beneath their bodies and I am frantic. I launch forward and fall to my knees, lavishing kisses and tears on Sven's face. The chair is still zip-tied to my ankles but I am closer to him.

"God, Sven, get up. Please," I beg. I push on his shoulder, terrified to touch Paul. Sven's eyes open slowly, one of them is swelling shut. "Oh my god, are you hurt?" I have never felt more panic in my life than this moment. Even with Paul taking me and threatening me, it was nothing compared to the fear that Sven may be dying. "Say something." I push on his shoulder again and he opens and shuts his eyes a few more times before straining to push Paul off of his chest.

The minute Paul rolls to his back on the blood-soaked carpet, I see the blood and my heart freezes. I sit back, covering my mouth as bile launches out of my stomach. I turn, vomiting on the floor. Hair hangs around my face, getting caked in vomit, and Sven gets up. He doesn't hold my hair, but he cuts my ankles loose from the zip ties.

When my stomach is empty, I use the back of my hand to wipe my mouth clean and push the hair out of my face. Sven came for me. He actually came even after I left him and told him I wanted nothing to do with him or his lifestyle. And my heart feels safe now with him here. Safer than I've ever felt, and not just because Paul is on the carpet in front of me bleeding out.

"Get up, we have to get out of here before the cops show up." Sven extends a hand to me, and I take it. I stand, and I have a strong urge to wrap my arms around him. Every bit of emotion I felt while sitting at Sarah's house talking to her bubbles up. I'm in love with this asshole to my very core, and I want to be with him.

"Sven," I start, but he's already heading toward the door. I glance down at Paul's bleeding form. "Is he going to die?" I ask, hurrying after him.

"Probably... If not he's going to prison anyway. They have a warrant out for him." Sven walks into the hallway and I follow, rubbing my wrists. They're raw but not bleeding.

"What about your gun?"

"Enough!" he snaps, glaring at me over his shoulder, and I bite my lip. I've hurt him too deeply. He stares at me for a long second and I wonder if I'll be able to repair what I broke or if it's too late. I'm not even thinking of Rico and the challenge of raising my son in a Bratva home. I just know I want him and I don't want to live without him.

I trail behind him all the way to his car. He pulls his phone out and sends several text messages as we descend the stairs. I am able to read the word "cleaner" and I see a street address he sends to someone. I'm not sure what that means other than he's cleaning up his mess, but it doesn't even bother me right now. After the hell I just went through, Sven's arms are the only place I can imagine feeling comfort again.

24

SVEN

Allie follows behind me as we walk. Tucker has already come and moved my car, followed me here when I sent out hasty messages for backup. Chances are my call for the cleaners to arrive will be a quick response too. And if Monroe can hold off Vice from serving the warrant, I'll have Allie safely away from this scene before the cops show their faces here. As long as no one called in the report of gunfire.

"Walk faster," I bark, feeling my chest so tight I can barely breathe. My job here is done. I killed the bastard who hurt her and avenged my family following the bullshit that man put me through. I have no more obligation to Allie than any other human on this planet. So why do I want to pull her into my arms and demand she never leave me?

"Sven, wait up," she calls, but I don't even look at her. I can't. When I see her face it makes me want her, and I thought she was a strength for me. It turns out, she's my greatest weakness.

"Walk faster," I snap again, picking up my pace. We're only a block away from Sarah's building, and that's where I'll leave her. Forever.

I hear rushed steps behind me and Allie jogs up to fall in step with me. I glance down at how she rubs her wrists; they're raw and almost bleeding. I've seen far worse injuries than this—compound fractures, bullet holes, lacerations that would make a doctor cringe. This is nothing, just a little rope burn, so why do I even give a single fuck about it? Except I force myself to resist the urge to take her into my arms and kiss every wound she has.

"Thank you," she mutters, sniffling. "He was going to kill me."

"I told you, you'd be safe with me. You left. What did you think was going to happen?" I round the corner of the building and see the uniforms out front. I recognize them immediately as friendlies, people Monroe probably called to make sure the building was secure after Allie was taken. Allie doesn't say anything else, though I sense she is hurt by my comment. She should have known better.

"Sven," one of the cops calls out, "is that the girl?" His chin jerks upward in Allie's direction. The younger cop is just naive enough to go along with anything the family says, which makes him perfect for grooming into a position of power with us.

"Yeah..." We stop and stand with the cops for a moment. Allie's eyes flit nervously, scanning their faces then looking down. She stands closer to me than she ever has; she's still afraid, or maybe it's something else. It doesn't matter. That part of the agreement ended the second she walked out of my house. I fulfilled my duties even though I didn't have to. And that is how I have to think of this.

"Monroe is up there. I think he's talking to CPS about the kid." The other cop I know less about, but Dominic trusts him. I nod and look up at the third story where lights stream out the windows. It's the only apartment still illuminated this time of night.

"I'm going up; watch for Tucker. He'll be bringing my car around." I gesture for Allie to follow me and open the door for her. I can tell there are unspoken words on her lips; her eyes are speaking volumes. It's easy to avoid eye contact with her since she follows me, but the real problem will come when Rico sees me. That kid pulls my damn heart strings so badly sometimes.

At the top of the stairs, I head toward Allie's apartment. Her shuffling footsteps are still there, trailing behind me. "Rico will be glad to see you back safe." I don't even knock on the door. If Monroe is here the door isn't locked. It swings open freely and I see Rico lying on the old squeaky leather sofa sleeping. Monroe and Sarah are seated at the kitchen table talking quietly, and Sarah pops to her feet, eyes wide, as Allie enters.

"Oh my god," she hisses and rushes around me. I turn to see Allie and Sarah hugging, Allie's eyes full of tears. "My god he hit you." Sarah lightly touches the wounds on Allie's face. Wounds I should be touching, cleaning, putting salve on. I feel my throat constrict and I clench my jaw.

"What the hell happened?" Monroe asks in a low voice. I match his volume, which I assume is so they don't wake the boy. I can see Allie's phone clutched in Rico's hand tightly. He snores softly, eyes darting beneath his eyelids.

"I used the address you gave me and I got to her before Vice. I'm pretty sure he's dead, but if not the courts can have fun with him." I look down at my shirt, soaked in his blood and clinging to my chest. "It got a little messy."

"I can see that," Monroe says, leaning in. "What the hell am I supposed to tell Vice?"

"Look, buddy, my cleaners are there. They'll make it look good, probably like someone robbed him of his stash. Gun is untraceable, left there at the scene. Allie's blood at the scene only proves she was taken by him, another count to add to his charges if he's alive. Go ahead and write up the report that she burst in here."

I eye Sarah and Allie harshly and they both look up at me. "She escaped from him before the robbery. And you go ahead and check her hands for gunshot residue. Prove she hasn't fired a weapon which means she's not the killer."

"Sven, this is a lot of fixing." Monroe mops his brow with his handkerchief and I notice Rico stirring on the couch. The boy turns over, mumbling something in his sleep. Allie's eyes still flow with tears but she nods at me gratefully.

"Please stay a bit," she whispers. "Rico will want to see you."

"It's better if I go." I move back toward the door and Monroe huffs out a sigh. "Got a problem?" I ask him, turning over my shoulder.

"Nah, get out of here." Monroe follows me to the door and shuts it. For a moment I stand outside the closed door thinking of what I am giving up. I invested a lot of energy and time into trying to make Allie mine, but I don't think it's a good fit anymore. My impulsivity and obsession with her make me think maybe I'm not cut out to have a partner like that. I head down the stairs with a hollow feeling in my chest and heavy feet. Each step thuds louder than the one before it until I'm on the sidewalk. I pass the uniforms and see Tucker with my car parked in the next block.

"Sven!"

Allie's shout guts me. I know she's just going to thank me politely for coming to save her. She made it clear that she won't have her son around my family and the lifestyle I live, so I'm not sure I even want to turn around. I keep walking toward my car pretending I haven't heard her when I hear her shoes slapping on the sidewalk.

"Sven, stop." Her hand grips my elbow and I turn to see her.

"What is it?" It might be the first time I've used a soft tone with her since we met. She's still crying, but this time it isn't fear in her bruised swollen eyes.

"I thought I could do this. I thought maybe I could walk away and start over and just be okay. That you were only using me for sex and that I could use you for protection the same way. I thought I'd go through with some fake marriage if Paul stuck around that long, that you'd get rid of him by chasing him away, and then I could divorce you and leave. And I was totally wrong, Sven. I can't leave you. And it's not because I need protection. It's because I love you."

She stares up at me with a quivering lower lip. It shakes so badly she bites it and I don't know what to say. No one besides Lacy has ever confessed to loving me. I'm an asshole. I'm a brute. I treat people like shit and capitalize on their willingness to submit to my authority and money. I'm not a lover, or compassionate.

"What are you saying?"

"I don't know. I just thought maybe you'd say. You love me too, that you feel something similar since we had all that time together." She's nervous, hesitating. I can see her withdrawing into herself again. She feels like a fool.

"What ever made you think that I am capable of love—the type of love you're confessing to having for me?" I study her eyes, then watch her facial expression change.

"You came for me." Allie steps closer to me, gingerly touching the blood on my chest. "You saved my life when you had no reason to."

"Paul attacked my men. It was just vengeance." My chest is tight. Her fingers tracing over my abdomen tingles my skin. I want her in my arms, but to say that would be to admit weakness. My enemies cannot see weakness in me, which means it cannot exist. I have to kill it.

"No, Sven. You told Paul you were doing it for me, because of what he did to me. You love me." She steps closer and rests her hand on my hip. "I don't know why you can't admit it, but I know you do."

I tense, squaring my shoulders. "You're wrong." I hate that she's right. I hate that part of me that defies my father and brother. It's supposed to die. I'm supposed to kill it. I'm supposed to be a trained killer with no inroads into my life whereupon my enemies travel.

"Sven!" Rico's voice meets my ears and I sigh, letting my chest deflate.

"You woke him?" I ask her, feeling like Samson the moment Delilah cut his hair, or Icarus the moment his wings began to melt.

"Sarah did... He asked for you." Allie looks up at the window of Sarah's apartment that overlooks the street and I follow her gaze with my eyes. Rico leans out the window. It's too far away to see his expression but because of his tone of voice, I know he's upset.

"Sven! Please come back. Please don't leave. Or take me with you. Please, Sven."

"My god," I grumble, feeling my mind changing without my consent. I'm a killer, not a lover.

"He loves you too, Sven." Allie slides her bloodied fingers between mine. "I will marry you, and we will raise Rico together. And we will shelter him from the family as much as we can."

"Sven, please, don't go," Rico sobs.

I look into Allie's eyes and realize I want that more than anything. This entire time it's all I have wanted, even when she was nasty and hateful toward me. I saw what I wanted and I went after it. "I'm a hitman, Allie."

"Do business out of a different office. Keep it out of the house. Marry me and protect me. That was the deal." Her tone is firm, but damn if that trembling lip isn't sexy.

"You're giving me orders now?" I ask, though I'm not upset by that. A dominant female is the only kind who survives the Bratva.

"Yes. Now, go get my things and our son and let's go home." She lets go of my hand, and the instant there is separation between us, I know I never want to feel it again. I grip her head between my large hands and pull her toward me, kissing her hard.

"My son?" I ask her, our foreheads pressing together.

"You've been more of a father to him than his own." Allie's hands rest on my biceps. "He needs a man in his life, just the way I do. Now are you coming with me, or should I have Tucker pick you up later?"

"God, you're hot when you're bossy." I kiss her again, harder this time, parting her lips. Her tongue dances across mine and I hear Rico upstairs cheering. Allie smiles against my mouth and leans into me.

"You like being dominated?" she asks in a cheeky tone, and I'm surprised to see her being so playful after the ordeal she's been through tonight. I put my hands on her waist and pull her against me hard.

"Does this mean anything to you?" I ask her, grinding my swelling cock against her abdomen. "Your sassy attitude and that snarky tongue you have really turn me on."

She rises up on her tiptoes and kisses me again, and when she lowers back to flat feet she looks serious. "Sven, I'm sorry for not believing you or trusting you. Paul really fucked me up. It took something this severe to make me see where I really belong."

I touch her bruised eye gently and shake my head. "That man was a complete monster. You deserve so much better, Allie. I just need to know that this is real now. That you're not going to change your mind when another bloody man comes walking through my front door. I lost Lacy; I won't make it if I lose you."

The confession would have me ousted from the family inner circle if my father heard it. So thank god my father isn't around here.

"I'm not changing my mind."

"What if it's just Stockholm syndrome?" I chuckle but she keeps her firm expression.

"I'm in love with you. Now take me home." She turns and calls over her shoulder to Rico, "Get your things! We're going home."

Rico shouts back, "Sven's house?"

"Yeah, buddy. Home... Odin misses you." I watch my words bring a priceless grin to his face and then he vanishes.

"But we're putting limits on his game time," she chides and I kiss her again. I have to leave the mothering to her, but I am thrilled they are coming back. I knew they belonged with me the whole time.

25

ALLIE

"And how are you enjoying everything today?" I ask the elderly couple seated near the window in the booth. The older woman looks up at me with rosy cheeks and pushes her glasses up on her nose.

"The food is delicious and the service is impeccable. Thank you so much." Her eyes sparkle as she talks, holding her husband's hand as if their physical connection is mandatory for her heart to keep beating. I can't help but be a bit jealous of that strong romantic connection, but what I have with Sven is unique. One day, maybe we will have that.

"Good to hear," I tell her as I walk away. After Dana took a job at a restaurant across town as head manager, I was promoted to assistant manager and tonight is my first shift. Sven and I had a good talk about me being able to work and now that Paul is gone, he doesn't feel the need to keep me locked up.

I walk toward the next table, ready to ask them how their food was when I see Sven walk in. He's alone, but I know his family will join him later. It's my shot at a few minutes to talk to him without anyone else around, so I make my way to him instead. He is stern as usual, but I smile at him and peck him on the cheek as I take his hand.

"Let's sit," I tell him, guiding him to a booth along the far wall. I nod at our new server Tonya and ask her, "Hey, can you keep things running? I'm going to have a break."

"Sure thing, boss," she says as she walks past, her brown ponytail swaying with each step. Sven and I sit in the booth where it's a bit quieter and I lace my fingers through his.

"How's the first day as boss?" He doesn't pull his hand away from mine, which is a subtle change. After three months of being together, Sven is starting to loosen up and understand the things that make me feel valued. He still hasn't opened up to me about what hurt him so badly that he can't show any emotion, and he hasn't told me he loves me yet, but we're making progress.

"Aw, it's okay. A lot like parenting a tween," I chuckle, though I'm serious. Being a boss isn't all it's cracked up to be but I enjoy the extra pay. Sven takes care of what I need, but I like to have that cash to spoil Rico now and then.

"I called the priest. He's booked for December thirteenth. We'll be married at St. Anne's and have our reception party at the Shadowbox."

I'm so glad he's helping take care of the wedding arrangements. Work has had me so busy I haven't had much time for it, though Sarah and I did pick out the most exquisite dress for my gown. I never saw myself as the type of woman who'd get married in winter but I want to marry this man more than anything, and I don't want to wait until next spring.

"That's good, so Dominic isn't fussing over things?" I know how much Dominic lectures Sven about his impulsivity. It's the same sort of lectures Sarah gives me sometimes, seeing as my mother and father are no longer in my life. Sarah has become my moral compass at times.

"Eh," Sven grunts, "Dom can fuck himself. He's leader of my work life, not my personal life." Sven brings my fingers to his lips and kisses my knuckles one by one. "You're mine. I'm allowed to have a life."

The gesture and the comment together make me want to climb onto his lap and feel his arms wrap around me, but I like this job and I want to keep it, so I settle for his lips on my hand. Dominic walks into the diner first, followed by Matty, then Rome. I don't see Leo anywhere, though he hasn't been around much lately. I wonder if he's still feeling guilty that he let his best friend plan a murder plot against his older brother.

"Hey, woah, none of that mushy stuff," Matty jokes, nudging Sven who scoots over. I stand and slide around to Sven's side and Matty sits next to me.

"Play nice, boys, this vixen might bite," Sven kids back, nudging me. I chuckle as Rome and Dominic take their place across from us. Family dinner together at the diner has become a bit of a tradition for Thursday evenings, and I'm enjoying getting to know his brothers. I only wish more of them would bring their partners around. Nanette, Dominic's wife, comes now and then.

"Where's Nan?" I ask, and Dominic shrugs.

"Had plans with her brother tonight." He scowls at Sven. "Heard from Leo? He's been MIA a lot lately."

Sven shakes his head. "Probably chasing tail. I hear Willow is back. Wonder what Dad will say?"

A darkness washes over the features of everyone at the table but me and I don't understand it, but I like to keep things light. "How about I go to the kitchen and get us all something—whatever's on draft." I nudge Matty and he slides out of the booth and lets me stand.

"Sure, but bring two for each of us. It's been a long day." Dominic nods at me and I wait, arms crossed over my chest. I'm going to whip these boys into shape one way or another. None of them have manners. I can really tell their mother died when they were young. Dominic stares at me for a moment, then sighs and adds, "Please and thank you."

Matty laughs at him and it brings a round of laughter to everyone. "Told you she's a vixen," Sven says and I wink at him before heading into the kitchen for the drinks.

Sven changed my life. He swept in to save me from a nasty customer and catapulted me into something I never saw coming. When I was a little girl I dreamed of growing up and making something of myself, finding Prince Charming and marrying him. I never expected what happened with Paul, or the struggle of being a single mother on the run. Sven is a light in my life that showed me fairy tales aren't real, but dreams can come true if you work hard enough.

As I get the drinks for my future husband and his brothers, I reflect on what family means. These boys have each other's backs and I get to be a part of this. More than anything, Rico gets to see first hand how a real family loves each other and protects each other. And that is something he would never have gotten from his own father. He's even started calling Sven dad now. I love it.

And I love that Sven has backed off from most of the dangerous parts of his family business for now. He's running the fish processing plant while Matty handles the scarier aspects of the gun business. The fact that Sven would make that sacrifice for me says "I love you" even when his lips don't say it.

Yeah, I'm pretty sure we were meant to be.

EXCERPT: DANGEROUS GAMES

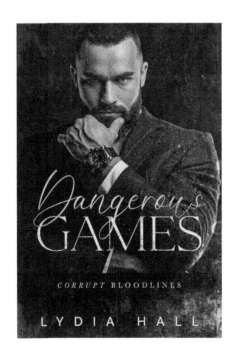

Rich, *powerful, cruel, older and dominant. I'm everything she hates... and everything she can't resist.*

Nanette Slater is my new hitman's sister. Unfortunately for the pretty brunette, her brother is no good at his job, which means Nanette ends up kidnapped and in my bed...

Unless he makes good on his promise, I'm keeping his sister to myself. Not that I'm complaining.

She's pretty irresistible despite the age gap, and the longer she spends in my home, the harder it is to resist her forbidden curves. I'm a man after all... A man her brother despises. But I'm not going to let that stop me.

Nanette's brother may think I'm a good for nothing criminal, but she makes her own decisions. And as soon as my dominant nature comes out, poor, pretty little Nanette is going to fall for me.

Hard.

DANGEROUS GAMES is the first book of The Corrupt Bloodlines series. This dark, sensual, twisted romance novel does *not* hold back on the spice!

Dominic

I sit in my car watching the house. He's in there with his sister, a union I won't disrupt for now, so long as he does what I tell him to do. But I won't wait long. Men like Jimmy Slater have a lot of skills but not a lot of loyalty, and if he tries to turn tail and run, I'll be in hot water, so I'm forced to sit on his tiny little craftsman home and wait until he's unoccupied. I've done this a few times; each time his sister is here, and God knows what she is trying to tell him or what he's told her.

The door opens, and the leggy brunette walks out. Her curly hair hangs around her thin, curvy frame. It's abnormal. She usually has it tied up, but today I get to enjoy her in all her splendor. She stands on the top step looking up at her brother and I admire that ass of hers, perky and tight, like she runs or something. It doesn't hurt that she is wearing heels and a pair of jeans that are so tight they look like they were painted on.

My cock twitches just looking at her. She is delectable, and I am a hungry man. I'd take a bite of that any time, but right now I can't be distracted. Not with the issues I'm facing. And Jimmy better come through for me, or maybe I'll end up finding a way to have my just desserts and a little icing on the cake. Nanette Slater could be just the icing I'm looking for.

She turns, stepping down the stairs, and looks right at my car. I know she can't see me; the windows are tinted too dark. But she has a scowl on her face. I wonder if Jimmy told her what he was up to, but he is smart. I've threatened him enough that he should know better. My business is private, and I don't usually have to tell people twice. What I've hired him to do is even more dangerous than a normal hit, and I've selected the best hitman in the city who isn't part of the family.

When Nanette is more than a block away, I step out of my car and button my coat. The piece conveniently holstered on my right hip is discreet. No one would know it's there if I don't tell them. But Jimmy will know. He knows who I am, and what I'm capable of.

The neighborhood is quiet, the sound of a lawnmower in the distance and some birds chirping is all I can hear. Jimmy won't be expecting me, though he should have something to report at least. The job shouldn't be taking this long. I gave him access to all my resources— the loyal ones anyway. And he has unlimited funds, courtesy of my credit card. There is no reason for him to be dawdling like this.

I jam my finger into the doorbell button and hear the chime on the other side of the door. Then I fold my hands in front of myself casually and wait. The smell of cat urine wafts up to my nose and I am disgusted. At least he could hose off his porch if he isn't going to chase the strays away. Jimmy has some poor hygiene habits when it comes to animals.

The door swings open and his face is buried in his phone. "What, Nan? You forget something?" His eyes sweep up to meet my gaze and they go wide. "Oh… Dom, hey, buddy. I'm, uh… I have."

"Move," I tell him, stepping across the threshold. He backs into his home frightened—as he well should be. He's taking too long, and he knows it. "Shut the door." I walk into his living room and stand directly beneath the light mounted in the center of the ceiling. The old area rug dampens my footsteps across the wood planks, but Jimmy's stockinged feet make no noise as he moves. A trained killer makes no noise when he moves; that's how I knew Jimmy was good at the first interview.

"Uh, Dom, I just. I'm sorry. I got delayed and—"

"Shut up." I look around the room. Everything is as it was the last time I came. He is less than a neat freak, but not a slob—except for the stray cats on the porch. The old home has seen better days though, a problem Jimmy could remedy if he just finished this job. He has a payout coming that's bigger than he's ever dreamed. "Tell me what you have."

His sniveling behavior is repugnant. He talks in circles, spouting things he told me last time. "The money all ties back to an offshore account. The payouts are going to someone named Henry Watts. He's a man of means, ex-military. I'm not sure—"

"Cut the crap, Jimmy." My voice startles him, and he jumps. By now he's got to have uncovered the truth about my identity. I never tried to hide it; I just didn't announce it before he accepted the job because men like him don't tend to get in bed with my type. At least not on their own accord.

"Dom, please, you have to understand that if I knew you were Bratva I'd have turned this job down. I'm not capable of this." He shoves his phone in his pocket and shakes his head, and it stirs my temper. He does not want to stir my temper.

"What did you say, Jimmy? I think you said you weren't going to do what you told me you'd do. Now if I remember correctly, I gave you some pretty nice compensation already. Access to every bit of intel I have. Unlimited funds. The power to even hurt me. And now you're backing out?" I take a step toward him, and he cowers, holding his hands up in a defensive posture.

"Dom, please. It doesn't have to go down this way, okay? I swear I won't tell a soul." He shakes his head as he backs into the wall and I advance on him slowly, a monster hunting his prey.

"You know that's not how this works, Jimmy. You are a smart man. You should have figured this out already." I unbutton my coat and pull out my Smith and Wesson and Jimmy literally whimpers. What a fucking coward. He calls himself a hitman? "Now, you are supposed to produce results for me. I need to know who hired the hit, and who is doing the hit. You have three days to figure this out, or you're not going to like me at all."

"Dom, woah," he says, his voice quavering. "Look, buddy, I'm not that good. At best I need two weeks, but this is tricky shit. I can't just tell you anything; I have to have the truth. That's what you want, right? Facts?"

I chamber a round and lean in so I know he hears me when I say, "Three days, Slater."

"That's insane. I can't do the—"

The gun goes off right next to his ear, firing a round through the wall and launching it into the wall on the other side of the adjoining kitchen. No doubt he'll find a hole in his siding out the back of the house. He winces, covering his ear and shouting. "Three days, Jimmy, or maybe we have a talk about writing your will."

"Fuck, what'd you do that for?"

"Consider it a friendly reminder that you are mine. You're on my payroll, which makes you just as guilty as me. You want to back out; well, I clean up all my mess. I don't leave loose ends hanging."

"God, Dominic, you have to understand I have a family too. I can't get wrapped up in this mess. I want a good life." He's busy rubbing his ringing ear when I bring the butt of my gun down hard on his shoulder, and he drops to his knees.

"Your family will appreciate that you are a hard-working man the instant you finish this job and give me what I want. You should have done your homework before accepting the job. Now you have three days to finish it, or—"

"I know, I know!" he shouts, which is the wrong move. My foot connects to his gut and he curls into a ball.

With my message sent, I slip out the front door as if nothing happened, and stroll to my car. At least it's a pleasant day. The sun is shining, and I have other business to tend to. So, when I climb into my car I head straight back to the office—my little slice of heaven in the back of the bookstore. I can't help but let my eyes linger on Nanette's ass as I pass her, now several blocks away and still walking. It sparks an idea in my mind of absconding with her and having my way in the back of my car, but business comes first.

I pull up to the bookstore and park in my usual spot. The boys are waiting for me; I'm certain of it. I was due in an hour ago, but Nanette took such a long time doing whatever it was with Jimmy that I had no choice. The instant I walk in I'm bombarded by questions. These guys are worse than a pack of yapping chihuahuas.

"Look, we've been waiting for an hour. What the hell happened?"

"Yeah, boss, there's a shipment coming, and we need your signature on the paperwork or—"

"Shut up," I snap, leading them into my office. I click on the lights and sit behind my desk. No one rushes me, and no one tells me how to do my job. Besides the fact that I can't tell them a single thing about Jimmy Slater or his task for me. This is an inside job; I know that much is true, and I don't have the means to sniff it out entirely by myself. Only, I don't know who to trust, who is loyal. "Sit down."

Nick and Leo sit across from me, both of them with resting bitch face, but I don't care. I'm in charge here and they do as I say. Nick crosses one leg over the other and leans back like he owns the joint, and Leo shakes his head, haughty and about to be taken down a notch. I unholster my gun, tucked there safely after I nearly made Jimmy deaf, and lay it on the desk. That sobers them and they look less hostile.

"The guns, they're due in tomorrow. Who is on that shipment?"

"We heard it's going to be the same guy as last time." Nick's report doesn't please me, but I'm not surprised. The Armenian arms dealer we work with has gotten sloppy and can't be trusted much longer.

"Put three extra men on it then. We can't afford a slip up. And Leo, I want you on the roof. Put the rifle on the truck. If something goes down, blow the tires first. If he doesn't stop, aim for his forehead." Leo nods, they understand my instructions and I know they will follow through, even if they are part of the problem here. "Now, where is the paperwork?"

Nick reaches into his jacket pocket and pulls out a folded bundle of papers. I take them and unfold them to see the order for seventy AR rifles is in order. I scrawl my name across the bottom and push the papers back to him, and he puts them back into his pocket. This crap is getting old, and I'm ready to move up, let my brother Sven take this over so I can do the real work of running this family, but only once I've proven my worth to my father.

"Get out," I tell them, ready to stew on my anger over Jimmy. They scurry away like scared little mice, and I sit back in my chair and listen to the door click shut. Someone in my organization has hired a man to kill me. I'm not sure if it is Nick or Leo. For all I know it could be one of my brothers too. They each have motive—to unseat me as the next Pakhan so they can take my rightful throne, though I don't truly suspect any of the four of them.

I pinch the bridge of my nose, breathing out a deep sigh. This stress isn't nearly as bad as some of the situations I've been in before, but it's right up there, and the only thing that takes the edge off is a good fuck. Too bad Nanette Slater is a little out of my reach at the moment, but if Jimmy doesn't play his cards right, I may just have to leverage her. She'd look really good bent over the end of my desk or spread wide on my bed. And just thinking of that makes my dick go hard.

I pull out my phone and flip through the pictures I took while I was waiting for Jimmy the last few times I showed up at his house. Nanette is in every single one of them, though some catch my eye more than others. Like this one where she's wearing a tight miniskirt. She dropped something and had to bend to pick it up, and as she did, I got a glimpse of the black panties she wore.

While Nanette is definitely worth feasting my eyes on, she's more valuable than that. Jimmy has a soft spot for her. I've seen it with my own eyes. She snapped at him about not feeding the strays and the very same day he removed the food dish from the front porch. Maybe I could use that weakness against him, force him to cooperate with me and maybe enjoy something I want on the side too.

Right now, Jimmy is a liability. He knows too much about me and my organization. If he were to rat, I'd go down, plain and simple. I need some insurance that he's going to do what I say, and Nanette might just be what I need. The minute he pulls that trigger, he will be just as guilty as me though, and that's what I'm counting on. Once he's done, he's done. He would go down as hard as I did if he ratted. And maybe Nanette could be just the thing to force him to finish what he started.

One thing is certain, I have to root out the mole and protect myself or there will be no organization left. At least not how it is today. My life depends on it, and so does my position in this family and I know Jimmy Slater is the only man who can do this. With my help of course. And maybe a little nudge from the goddess he calls his sister.

Read the complete story HERE!

SUBSCRIBE TO MY EXCLUSIVE NEWSLETTER

I hope you enjoyed reading this book.

If you want to stay updated on my upcoming releases, price promotions, and any ARC opportunities, then I would love to have you on my mailing list.

Subscribe yourself to my exclusive mailing list using the below link!

Subscribe to Lydia Hall's Exclusive Newsletter

Printed in Great Britain
by Amazon

36449390R00121